Katha Sagar
Ocean of Stories

Hindu Wisdom for Every Age

By Sarah Conover
With Abhi Janamanchi
Illustrations by Shanthi Chandrasekar

Skinner House Books
Boston

www.skinnerhouse.org

Printed in the United States

Illustrations by Shanthi Chandrasekar

ISBN: 978-1-55896-776-2

6 5 4 3 2 1
18 17 16

Library of Congress Cataloging-in-Publication Data

Names: Conover, Sarah, author. | Janamanchi, Abhi, author.
Title: Katha sagar, ocean of stories : Hindu wisdom for every age / By Sarah Conover With Abhi Janamanchi.
Description: Boston : Skinner House Books, 2016. | Includes bibliographical references.
Identifiers: LCCN 2016000334 | ISBN 9781558967762 (pbk. : alk. paper)
Subjects: LCSH: Hindu stories. | Hindu legends. | Hindu mythology.
Classification: LCC BL1146.C66 K38 2016 | DDC 294.5/432--dc23 LC record available at https://lccn.loc.gov/2016000334

Acknowledgments

I'd like to thank Mary Benard and the rest of the staff at Skinner House Books for their patience and good faith in the worthiness of this project; Lalitha Janamanchi for her rigorous attention to the essential details of village life for our South Indian storyteller; Varadarajulu Rengapashyam and Girija Rengapashyam for overwhelmingly generous hosting during my stay in Chennai, India; my husband, greatest fan, and most candid reviewer, Doug Robnett; and finally, my steadfast collaborator on this multi-year adventure, Abhi Janamanchi—may our work together bear some fruit of understanding and appreciation among peoples of the world.

Sarah Conover

Books by Sarah Conover

Kindness: A Treasury of Buddhist Wisdom for Children and Parents

Daughters of the Desert: Stories of Remarkable Women from Christian, Jewish, and Muslim Traditions
with co-authors Claire Rudolf Murphy, Meghan Nuttal Sayres, Mary Cronk Farrell, and Betsy Wharton

Ayat Jamilah, Beautiful Signs: A Treasury of Islamic Wisdom for Children and Parents
with co-author Freda Crane

Harmony: A Treasury of Chinese Wisdom for Children and Parents
with co-author Chen Hui

Chaos and Wonder and the Spiritual Adventure of Parenting: An Anthology
with co–editor Tracy Springberry

Muhammad: The Story of a Prophet and Reformer

Table of Contents

Preface

This is a book of stories selected from ancient Hindu epics, myths, and folk traditions of India. Many were handed down to Abhi by his mother, grandparents, aunts, uncles, and teachers. In choosing and arranging them for you we have tried to be faithful to the traditional versions told throughout India. The stories convey key values, like honesty, generosity, devotion, and justice, and introduce some basic religious and cultural observances. The images, sounds, tastes, smells, and textures of the land, animals, and people are those that surrounded Abhi and his wife, Lalitha, in southern India, and are an integral part of the narrative.

Thousands of years in their telling and creative retelling, these stories invite you to explore one of the world's most ancient and varied religious traditions and the cultures shaped by it. The settings and characters—worldly and otherworldly—are some of the lenses through which a Hindu experiences the world. Vivid dramas involving gods, kings, sages, and fools offer consideration of life's biggest questions—birth, death, human purpose, and meaning. Through the interdependence of all creation in the stories, Hinduism's awe of and wonder about the universe are revealed.

The stories are told by a fictional *pauranika* named Lakshmi, a professional storyteller who lives in a small South Indian village. Pauranikas are living treasuries of sacred myths and epics, wisdom and folk tales, values and traditions. Trained in classical music and dance, they intersperse their performances with music, dance, drama, and sub-stories. These stories are told in temples and homes, in villages and cities alike. In villages, a local temple or some other communal place may be used for performances; in larger towns, they may be held in auditoriums and community centers.

In Western culture, stories often tend to convey a message, support an idea, strengthen an argument, or make a point. In the Hindu tradition, however, the story itself is the point. Stories are intended not as explanations of the world but as experiences of that which is eternal, enduring, and enriching. We hope you will personalize these stories by imagining yourself as the characters experiencing theses events.

The back of this book contains three resources that you may find helpful to look at as you go along: a section titled "On Hinduism" that will deepen your understanding of this religion and explain some of the major distinctions between it and many others; "Story Notes and Resources" providing context; and a glossary of terms. That peoples of the world can see the world so very differently from one another in their ideas about the Divine is extraordinary, and the very first insight necessary for becoming a world citizen. We invite you to keep an open, curious, and reverent mind on this pilgrimage.

Sarah Conover and Abhi Janamanchi

Katha Sagar

The Pauranika

 At last, the relentless monsoon rains of summer end. Rivers, swollen and furious, race from the mountains to the sea. The rays of the long-missed sun wedge through the tangled jungles bordering every village, waking all of creation with light. Claiming small kingdoms, the *koels*, cuckoos, sing one over another while the last drops of water on their feathers vanish with the dawn. The lowing of cows, oxen, and buffalo fills out the bass notes of the chorus.

Giddy children spill out of the doorways and run into the sunshine. On this first day of clear-blue skies, they know to seek out their *pauranika*, their village storyteller, Lakshmi, for she will have some special tales to celebrate the day. And maybe tonight, they hope, she will begin a days-long story from one of the holy epics—the Ramayana or the Mahabharata, the Vishnu Purana or the Shiva Purana.

Rising from her bed, Lakshmi, the storyteller, smiles at the hubbub of creatures. Out her window she glances at the rain-plump rice fields blazing green in the daylight. "Hunger will gain no foothold this year!" she says aloud to herself.

She showers, dries off, dresses in a sky-blue sari, then examines her face in the mirror, chuckling at her wrinkles—the tiny bird feet that have perched at the edges of her eyes. Opening a small ceramic pot, she dips an index finger in the vermilion powder to make a bright red tilak, a small decorative circle, on her forehead between her eyebrows—the tradition of Hindu women from ancient times. Tilting her head, she brushes her long, black hair one side at a time before braiding it, noticing that the fine strands of silver are multiplying. Because they show the gift of years, she is grateful for each one.

Next, Lakshmi takes a few minutes to complete the daily puja, her home worship, and then steps outside. From the flower garden just beyond the front door, she fills her basket with blossoms. Today, Friday, is an auspicious day, and she will pay a visit to the village temple with her collection. Only a few minutes' walk from home, the temple's granite walls look more a part of nature each year, shrubs and vines sprouting from the crevices in the mortar. But as soon as she nears the temple *mandap*, or pavilion, the village children spot her and she's surrounded. They tug at her sari, jostle and cajole her, until she can make no further progress forward. "Tell us a story, Amma!" they say, calling her Mother as they do all the older women in the community. "Tell us a really good story, but not too long, because our parents are expecting us home for breakfast!"

Lakshmi looks down at eager faces. The young adults—including her youngest son and daughter—have abandoned the village to pursue jobs in the big cities, so she knows it to be her life's task, before these young ones disappear, to make sure they carry within them an ocean of stories to see them through life. Just like the gods and goddesses, heroes and heroines in the epics, they will have lives full of encounters with good and evil, triumph and trial, courage and fear. Lakshmi believes one thing is certain: Good will always find ways to prevail—if not this year, then in ten years, or three hundred. If not in this world, then in another.

Since the beginning of time, and even before time existed, from the end of time and back again, the ancient tales have pointed a way forward. The wicked seek to hoard riches and power, while the good choose to share them, often retreating to the simplicity of the forest. The righteous king brings justice and prosperity to the people; the greedy king brings mayhem and suffering. The farmer, herder, parent, and grandparent who attend to duty, their *dharma*, flourish, while those who neglect virtue reap painful *karma*, the bitter fruit of their actions.

Certainly the storyteller can recall many short stories written in the holy books, the Vedas, but she can also recite the epics by heart in their entirety, all twenty-four thousand verses of the Ramayana and the hundred thousand stanzas of the Mahabharata, just as the mothers in her family have done since anyone thought to take note of the century. Lakshmi had heard these stories before she was born, but her formal training by her grandmother began at age seven. It took her eleven years to master the pitch and tone of the holy stories, and at least that long to bring them to life through music and dance.

An outsider might think that nothing much ever happens in this village. But everyone here knows better and would tell you that right now, in their village, just like in the place you live, stories are continually conjured, repeated, revised, and told anew, and that each and every creature forges its own unique life's tale.

So many stories in Hinduism, one inside the other, and every link leading to a different tale, each layered with wisdom and foolishness, good and evil, generosity and greed. Lakshmi has no doubt that the stories were created from the breath of the Divine. Only the supreme

God, Brahman, is beyond story, beyond shape, words, and time. Brahman manifests on earth as a holy Trinity: Brahma, the Creator; Vishnu, the Sustainer, who descends to earth from time to time as an *avatar*, a divine teacher to save humanity from its biggest mistakes; and Shiva, the Destroyer in order that the world may renew itself. In addition to this trinity there are the minor gods and goddesses, who together number thirty-three million!

But who can really say how many gods there are and how they came to be? Who can say how any of us came to be? Perhaps, after listening to Lakshmi's stories, you might suspect that gods and goddesses and heroes and heroines are not so long ago and far away in other lands but born amongst us still to fight for good. You might even suspect that you could be one of them, battling to keep virtue alive in yourself as well as in others.

The world evolves, every victory is temporary, and thus the stories can never end, can they?

The village children, delighted in their successful demands for a story, quickly find a place on the steps of the mandap. Today being a holiday, fieldwork will be halted for a time to celebrate the end of the rains. Cheerfully the pauranika surrenders, puts aside her flower basket, and settles down on the topmost step. The sun has risen high enough so that all the youths—and a few adults too—scramble for a place on the steps or close by in the shade of a nearby banyan tree. When all are settled, even the littlest child is silent in anticipation.

"Because we revere Mother Nature," begins Lakshmi, "and She has, once again, freely given us the rains we need to grow crops, let us celebrate Her, She who provides." Lakshmi's gaze lifts above her audience to admire the protection of the banyan, branches and roots spreading so widely that twenty elephants could shade themselves beneath it.

The pauranika smiles. "Let us hear the story of the miracle of the banyan tree." She begins with a *sloka*, a traditional chanted prayer from one of the Hindu holy books, the Upanishads:

asatoma sadgamaya,
tamasoma jyotirgamaya,
mrityorma amritangamaya,
Om shanti, shanti, shanti.

Lead us from untruth to truth,
from darkness to light,
from mortality to immortality.
Peace, Peace, Peace.

Repeated aloud until everyone joins in, the prayer runs its course.

The Miracle of the Banyan Tree

 Many centuries ago, a wise man named Uddalaka wanted to teach his son a lesson about one's true nature. One day in late summer, when the banyan tree's red fruit ripened, he said to his son, "Svetaketu, go and pick a single fruit from our tree and bring it back here."

"Yes, Father," replied the boy. Because the banyan was ancient, many of its roots draped from branch to ground like bridges of rope. Svetaketu eyed the tree and tucked the long folds of his white *dhoti*—the unstitched cotton cloth worn by men and boys—around his waist. Now he could climb.

He hopped on one of the banyan roots to a branch, shimmied up the trunk, and searched among the big heart-shaped leaves for the small fruit. He found a cluster, but chose only one fruit, as his father had asked. Stowing it into a pleat in his dhoti, the boy slid down the smooth bark and ran back with his small prize in hand.

Uddalaka did not take the fruit from the boy but gestured for him to hold on to it. "Break it open, Son, and tell me what you find inside." The boy did as he was told, squashing the fruit between thumb and forefinger.

The remains spread in his palm, Svetaketu fingered through them. "I see some tiny seeds, Father."

"Well, then, break one of the seeds open and tell me what you see inside that," said his father.

This task proved more difficult—the boy pressed a small, hard seed between two finger-nails until it crushed into a speck on his fingertip. Svetaketu frowned and studied it, bewildered. "Nothing at all, Father. There is nothing left."

Looking from Svetaketu's hand to the towering tree, the sage said, "Yes, Son. It seems like nothing at all, doesn't it? But from that tiny seed, a giant tree grows." He paused so that they could appreciate the fact and listen to the birds clustered in the tree's topmost heights.

"That nothing on your fingertip is the real, Svetaketu," said the father, "what we call Brahman, God, the invisible at once everywhere and in everything—the unseen behind the stars' glimmering, the banyan trees' stretching toward light, and the birds' caroling. Brahman is the real. You are that too, my son."

Svetaketu contemplated these words from his father. He took a deep breath and sighed. He was a young boy and some things, he knew, would take time to truly understand.

The sage looked at his son's puzzled face, chuckled, and took his hand. "When we try to locate God exactly—inside a seed or even inside of us—it can't be grasped or held. It is beyond form," said Uddalaka. "Within you, that spark of Brahman is the very one peering out through your eyes!"

Lakshmi ends her story, but no one stirs to leave. After their early morning bab-
ble, the birds quiet down. A child sneezes. A toddler fusses until his older brother
reaches down and picks him up. "Amma," asks a girl, "is Brahman so small that we
can't see it, or so big that we can't see it?"

The pauranika grins. "Yes. Just like that!"

"But how did big and small happen? Tell us that story, Amma."

"Oh, you are asking such a big question for a small person!" says Lakshmi.
"There are many stories and ideas about the beginning, but not even those astro-
nauts who circle our earth in their little spaceships know the answer to this biggest
of mysteries. How did it all begin? Perhaps it's a forever riddle." The pauranika
brushes a fly off her arm, then rests her hands back in the lap of her sari. "Let's
start with one that makes me laugh when I try to picture it."

Brahma and Vishnu

There was a time when the Three Worlds did not exist—not Deva Loka, the realm inhabited by heavenly beings called *devas*, or Bhoo Loka, the earthly realm of humans, or Asura Loka, the realm of the *asuras*, power-seeking beings we call demons, who oppose and compete with the gods.

In the utter darkness, Lord Vishnu, who maintains and protects the world, rested on a magnificent serpent—the thousand-headed Sesha—in the middle of the Cosmic Ocean. So unperturbed and peaceful was Vishnu that out of his navel grew a perfectly formed lotus.

But along came the Creator of the Three Worlds, Lord Brahma, who drew near Vishnu and whispered in his ear, "Tell me, who are you?"

Vishnu opened his dream-filled eyes and answered, "I am the Creator of the Universe. All the worlds, and even you yourself, are inside me." Vishnu began to drift back asleep, but suddenly his eyes snapped open again. "By the way, who are *you?*"

Brahma replied, "*I* am the Creator and everything is inside *me*."

Lord Vishnu then entered Lord Brahma's body and found that, indeed, the Three Worlds were inside his belly.

Amazed, Vishnu exited through Brahma's mouth and said, "Now you must enter my belly in exactly the same way and see the Three Worlds—heaven, earth, and hell."

Brahma, never one to argue, did as he was asked. When he went deep within Vishnu's body, he, too, found the Three Worlds inside. By that time, however, Vishnu had closed his mouth.

Nevertheless, Brahma found another way out—right through Vishnu's navel. He landed atop the lotus, where he decided to stay, where we can always find him if we use our imagination.

The storyteller sees some of the children squeezing their eyes shut, trying to picture this. She smiles and does the same. "Oh, I think I see them. The sea is vast and made of . . . milk! And Vishnu, deep blue as the bluest sky, naps untroubled on the mighty snake, Sesha. And there's Brahma, all finished with the world's creation, and very tired now, curled up and napping in the middle of Vishnu's belly-button lotus." A few of the youths giggle.

"But wait," says Lakshmi, opening her eyes, "another story is rising up from the Cosmic Ocean. This one is not so clear at first." She closes her eyes, and the children follow her example.

The Egg of the Universe

 In the beginning, nothing at all existed. Nothing at all—not a single sound, not a blink of light, not the shadow of a bug. Imagine!

After a time, for no reason we can understand yet, the cosmos began to warm, and something began to grow. The cosmos became even hotter, more than boiling hot, and deep within that something an egg grew.

Drifting about in the boundless cosmos, the egg lay dormant for the time of a single year. After a year, the egg broke open into two halves: one silver, the other gold.

The silver half became this earth that we rest on, and the golden half became the sky over our heads. The thick egg white mounded into the world's first mountains, the transparent membrane of the yolk became the mist and clouds, and the small veins within the yolk flowed as the earth's many rivers. Lastly, the fluid of the yolk grew into the many seas and oceans.

What was born next? The sun! And at its birth, the joyous shouts and hurrahs of all desires and all beings rose up toward it, just as flowers grow toward sunlight. And when the sun rises every single day, again more shouts and hurrahs rise up to it, and that is why the birds are so noisy in the morning!

Finishing the myths, Lakshmi sends everyone on their way to their breakfasts. In the silence that follows, she enters the temple and places the flowers at the shrine. She finishes her prayers in the windowless half-light, grateful for the holiday and the chance to start the day with a few stories before everyone begins their chores.

The Dhoti

 Once there lived a *guru*—a spiritual teacher—and his student near a village. They spent their hours praying and meditating in a tiny hut without chairs, tables, or beds—just a dirt floor with a few straw mats for sleep. They ate only what food the villagers offered them for their holy devotions.

One day, the teacher beckoned his disciple and said, "My son, I am leaving on a pilgrimage to the Himalaya Mountains and will be gone for a couple of years. Remember all that I have taught you. Attend to the villagers' spiritual needs, and help when you can. Above all else, strive to lead a simple life, for simplicity is the guardian of your goodness and virtue."

The disciple touched his teacher's feet as a gesture of respect and made a promise to do so. Pleased by the young man's vow and devotion, the guru blessed him and left.

A day later, the young man washed his spare *dhoti*—an unstitched white cloth that men and boys wear—and hung it out to dry outside the hut. After his morning prayers, he set out to the village to beg for food. Receiving some rice and vegetables, he then returned to his hut in order to cook the food and eat it.

As the student was about to enter the hut, he noticed a rat scampering around with a piece of white cloth in its mouth. The rag looked familiar. It was . . . his dhoti! "Oh no!" he cried. "The rats have torn my spare dhoti to shreds. I will have to beg for another!"

The next day, during his daily rounds, the young man stopped at the house of the village elder. "Respected Sir, I need a dhoti. Might you have an extra?" he asked.

"A dhoti? Why would you need a dhoti instead of food?" asked the elder.

"The rats got my spare dhoti and tore it to shreds. I'll need another so that I can always wear a clean one."

Said the elder, "I have a brand new dhoti. It would bring spiritual merit to my family to give it to one who lives a life of purity." He went into the house and came back with a new silk dhoti. When the young man saw it, he felt thrilled to receive not just a new dhoti but a silk one. He stood there, fingering it, for he had never touched any cloth but the roughest cotton before.

As the young man returned to his hut with his expensive gift, he pondered the rat problem and wondered how he could prevent a rat from devouring the silk dhoti, for surely a lucky prize like this would never fall into his hands again. He decided to get a cat.

The following day on his alms rounds, he begged for a cat. A family that had a dozen cats gladly gave him one. Soon enough, just as the young man had hoped, the rats went elsewhere.

But it wasn't long before the student realized that he needed to keep the cat well fed so it would continue to guard the hut against rats. So he decided he must somehow get a cow to milk. Learning that the richest man in the village was donating cows to the poor, the young man showed up at his mansion and received a plump cow.

The cow provided plenty of milk for the cat and the young man. He no longer needed to beg for food—and besides, he didn't have all that much time for meditating and prayers anymore, as caring for the animals took up most of his days.

He soon realized, however, that the cow needed fresh straw every day in order to provide milk. He thought about it and decided to build a fence and cultivate a patch of land near his hut for this purpose.

The student collected some wood and twine for the fence, and borrowed some seeds from a neighbor to plant. He soon found himself watering the field and tending to the seedlings all day. A few months later, he was rewarded with an abundant harvest. Once the grain was harvested, he was left with an ample supply of straw for his cow.

But now he had more grain than he needed. So the young man decided to build a barn to hold the extra straw and grain. However, he had more grain than the barn could hold, so he soon found himself in the business of selling the grain and making a handsome profit.

With the money, he was able to hire laborers to work in his field and replace the tiny hut with a nice house. Too busy now from dawn until night to pray, the young man could barely keep up with the field hands, carpenters, and servants he'd hired. The young man said to himself, "I need someone to share my life with, who will manage my affairs." He inquired in the village and married a virtuous young woman. They were well suited for one another, and soon enough, they were a family of four.

One fine day, the guru returned from his pilgrimage to move back in with his student. Weary from traveling for months on foot and begging for sparse food along the way, he arrived at the spot where he remembered his hut to be situated. In its place, however, stood a beautiful two-story house surrounded by flower gardens, vegetable gardens, coconut groves, a herd of cows, a large barn, and many laborers attending to all the enterprises. Adjoining the house, lush green rice paddies stretched all the way to the village.

"Am I in the right place?" wondered the guru. "Where is my little hut? What happened to my poor disciple?" He began to get upset. "Did some rich man drive him away and build his estate here?"

Just then, a servant came out of the house and inquired what the sage wanted.

"My good man," the sage said, wide-eyed, "a young student devoted to a life of purity and poverty lived here once. Do you know where he is now? Is he safe?" Before the servant could respond, the young man, hearing the voice of his teacher, rushed out of the house and fell at his guru's feet.

"Guru-ji, welcome! I am so glad to see you! How have you been? How was your pilgrimage?" he asked.

"My son, what has happened here?" asked the guru with bewilderment writ large on his face. "I left you leading a simple, holy life, and I return to find you surrounded by more wealth and possessions than you can keep track of."

"Ah, Guru-ji . . . It's a long story that began with an old dhoti the day after you left! To protect it from the rats, I needed a cat, and then the cat needed food, and then . . . well, there seemed to be no end to the various needs and wants . . . "

Frowning, the guru replied, "And so, my son, you have joined the ways of the world and forgotten that your simple life was rich in time and peace! Yes, you are a wealthy man now, but so busy that your heart is starving. Is contentment the thing you will try to buy next?"

On this morning, the air feels crisp and clean to Lakshmi—she welcomes it through the open doors and windows. Later, to keep out the sun's burning rays when the temperature rises, she will shutter the windows, but keep the doors ajar to the breeze.

Lalitha appears bright and early in the large kitchen. The pauranika reminded her before bed last night that today would be the birthday of Lalitha's deceased but beloved great-great-grandfather. In honor of that fact, Lakshmi might have a before-school story for her.

"Namaste, Grandmother!" Lalitha says. Already bathed, with coconut oil combed through her long hair to keep it silky and dressed in her school uniform, she stands at eager attention. Lakshmi points to the table so Lalitha will take a seat to be served her breakfast before any story. She puts before the child a plate of two idlis—steamed rice cakes mixed with ground lentils—and a small metal bowl of coconut and coriander chutney.

Needing no silverware, Lalitha pours the green chutney on her plate and pushes some of it around in circles with a piece of the rice cake. A look of bliss appears on her face when she starts chewing.

Watching her eat, Lakshmi asks, "What do you remember of your great-great-grandfather, Lalitha?" They both look up at the photograph of him on the wall. Lakshmi had earlier placed a small table before his image with an offering of a lit sesame oil lamp and a stick of incense.

"He was very old? That's what I remember."

The storyteller laughs. "What else? What is he best remembered for in the village?"

"Oh! That he was very generous and kept a vow his whole life never to eat on a day he hadn't fed a poor and hungry person!"

"Right you are," says the pauranika. "I admired him so much. Even though he was a successful businessman, his real wealth was his goodness."

"Didn't he stop robbers one time, Grandma?" Lalitha asks, starting on her second rice cake.

"Well—yes and no. He wasn't exactly there. My grandmother and her sisters were headed to the city on their cart when robbers overtook them. But when the bullock cart driver told the thieves the family's name, they gave everything back right away. 'We don't rob that family,' they said. 'They are very good to many!' So in a way my grandfather was actually there, don't you think?"

"Uh huh," Lalitha mumbles with a last mouthful of food.

Her grandmother takes the empty plate away and sits down beside her. "Turn your chair so that your back is to me, Lalitha. I will braid you a story and I will also braid your hair. Maybe you have heard this before," says the pauranika, "but even so, every time I tell it I find myself thinking about it for a long time, and it reminds me of my grandfather. Ready?"

Heaven and Hell

Once, long ago, a man named Amul, scorched from the summer sun, sat under a large pipal tree to rest in its shade. As it was lunchtime, it occurred to him that he was quite hungry. He had the thought that he would like nothing better than a cold mango *lassi*, a sweet yoghurt drink. The lassi instantly appeared in his hand, chilled perfectly, condensation dripping down the sides of the glass. Surprised but delighted, Amul drank every bit. Soon after, he found himself wishing that he could snack on a masala dosa, a warm crepe made of rice and lentils and filled with potatoes, onions, and spices. The dosa, steaming, appeared on a plate before him. He gobbled it down, smiling all the while. He thought next about some *dal*—lentil stew—and perhaps some steaming rice to mix in it. All these appeared: the dal heaped in a bowl and the rice on a silver plate beside it.

Amul grinned. "What's this?" he said aloud. "Everything I desire appears as soon as I think of it! This must be a very special tree indeed—a wish-fulfilling tree—for this has never happened to me before!" He decided not to move from his spot. Amul stayed the night, the whole next day, and another night, eating whatever he wished and as much as he wished.

Finally, though, he thought that he should return home and see about his family. Yet he did not want to leave this astonishing tree! Is this just like heaven, he wondered? He could live the rest of his life here and never need to labor for food again! Overwhelmed by such an important decision, he thought that perhaps a holy man could tell him the right thing to do, and of course, instantly a man appeared and stood in front of him.

Bone-thin, dressed in only a loincloth, with long dreadlocks like the god Shiva, the man asked, "What is it you want, brother?"

"Are you really a holy man, a sage?" Amul asked.

"I have dedicated my life to the path of wisdom, so some would say so," he answered. "What is it that I may do for you?"

Amul thought for a bit, unsure. Finally, thinking that he might already be in heaven, he asked, "Is this heaven? My desire is to see heaven." He saw that the holy man did not flinch at this request. "But," Amul continued, "I want to come back to this spot. I want to see heaven and then return right here."

Unsmiling, the holy man said, "I can lead you to heaven, but know that the road there leads through hell first. It's one and the same road. You can't travel to heaven without passing through hell."

Amul considered. "Well," he thought to himself, "it can't be so different than traveling through a poor country to reach a rich one, can it?" He felt very clever. "All right, then," Amul said. "I'll do it. Please take me."

The sage sat down next to Amul and they both vanished from under the tree. Away they went down the secret road to hell and heaven. They landed in hell at noontime, the exact time of day Amul had arrived at the pipal tree a few days earlier. Before them, they saw a table laden with every delicious food Amul had ever seen and many more he couldn't have even dreamed of: savory curries of every color, stuffed vegetables, rice biryanis, dal, chutneys, and potatoes, as well as laddoos, jalebis, coconut halwa, and every sweet he had imagined eating as a young boy but could never afford.

Amul's fascination was interrupted by the clanging of a loud bell. Daing! Daing! Daing! Hundreds of people, scrawny and thin, raced to the table, necks craned toward the feast, arms stretched to grab the food. Each had long, long wooden spoons called *uddharini* bound to their arms and wrists. Because of the uddharini, they could not use their hands to eat. They scooped up food in the bowls of the spoons, but the uddharini were so long that they could not get a morsel to their mouths. Starving, they dashed around the table; lentils flew through the air, heaps of rice landed underfoot, sweets rolled away. Not a single bite landed in a single mouth.

Daing! Daing! Daing! rang the bell again. "Lunch is over," boomed a loud voice. Still desperately hungry and further exhausted, the hordes reluctantly turned and walked away.

Amul's eyes widened and his face paled. Neither man moved but only watched sadly as the hungry, looking like walking bones, dispersed.

The sage turned toward the stunned Amul. "This is hell," he said. "No matter that they have every delicious food in the world heaped high on a table that groans under its weight, they leave even hungrier than before. Now, let's go visit heaven."

Away they flew to heaven, where it was also time to eat. The lunch bell clanged the moment the two of them arrived. Daing! Daing! Daing! Just like in hell, the tables, piled with mountains of the same delicious food they had seen before, stretched as far as the eye could see. As people approached, Amul noticed with alarm that they, too, had uddharini bound to their arms so that they could neither grasp the food with their fingers nor bring it to their mouths. Amul turned his gaze away, not wanting to witness such suffering again.

"Eat!" a voice boomed. But the crowd did not rush to feed themselves. Instead, cheerful voices erupted. Amul looked. Each person hunted for some choice morsel, but lifted the food with his or her uddharini and turned to feed another! The sticks made it easy for one person to feed the next, and the next to feed someone else.

And in this way, sharing the food, giving it to one another, all were fed. The platters were emptied with neither a grain of rice wasted nor a single sweet dropped to the floor. By the time the next bell rang to signal the end of lunch, stomachs were full and faces grinning. Full of joy, friends one and all, they turned from the tables and went on their way.

The sage looked at Amul, who was gazing at the scene with an understanding nod. The holy man clasped Amul's hand and they soon found themselves back beneath the wish-fulfilling pipal tree.

"You see?" said the holy man. "Hell and heaven are right here on earth, all the time. It is so very simple: What you receive, you must also give. If you only think of your own happiness, you will never, ever be happy."

Amul, much the wiser, placed his two hands together in a grateful bow of respect and headed home to his family.

Yudhishthira's Wisdom

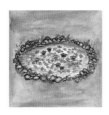 King Yudhishthira, the eldest of the five Pandava princes, was beloved for his commitment to truth and duty over worldly ambition. One day, he and his brothers went for a hunt in the forest. Pursuing a deer, they wandered deep into unfamiliar territory. By mid-afternoon the sun was blazing overhead and they had grown tired and very thirsty. The deer was nowhere to be seen, so footsore and weary, the brothers decided to rest for a while in the shade of a tree.

Yudhishthira first dispatched Sahadeva, the youngest brother, in search of water. He went readily enough, but when he did not return for a long time, Yudhishthira grew concerned. He then sent Nakula, the fourth brother, to see what had happened to the youngest. Nakula obeyed, yet he too did not return. Yudhishthira sent his remaining brothers, Arjuna and Bhima, after the first two. When none returned, he grew very anxious, not knowing what had befallen them. So Yudhishthira decided to go and see for himself.

Following their footsteps, he walked on for a distance until he came to a pond in a clearing. The still waters reflected the blue sky, while the pink, white, and blue lotuses that grew in it raised their smiling heads toward the sun. But as the king's eyes swept over the peaceful scene, he beheld another sight that filled him with grief: By the banks of the pond, his four brothers lay cold and still, seemingly dead. Sorrow filled the king's heart and he fell on his knees and wept bitterly for them, crying out to heaven to take him too, for he could not live without his brothers.

Eventually, Yudhishthira was overpowered by his thirst. As he knelt upon the bank and bent down to scoop some water in his hands, a voice broke through the silence. "Stop, O King," said the voice. "This is my pond. You may not drink the water until you have answered my questions. If you dare to disobey, you will face the same fate as your brothers."

"Who are you?" called Yudhishthira, looking around.

"I am a yaksha," the voice replied, "a spirit, the caretaker of this pond. "Ask your questions. I shall answer them as well as I can," said Yudhishthira.

The spirit continued, "It is well for you that you heeded my warning. Now listen to my questions. What makes the sun shine?"

"The power of God!" Yudhishthira answered.

"What is a person's surest weapon against danger?" asked the yaksha.

Yudhishthira answered, "Courage!"

"What feeds and sustains people and makes them strong?" the yaksha persisted.

Without hesitation, Yudhishthira said, "A mother, surely. A mother gives us life and feeds and sustains us."

"When does a person become beloved?" asked the spirit.

Yudhishthira responded, "When a person gives up pride."

"What is that which makes people happy when they have lost it?"

"Anger," responded Yudhishthira.

"What can one give up and immediately become rich?"

"Desire," answered Yudhishthira.

So it went on, until at last the yaksha said, "I am well pleased with your answers, and I shall restore to you one of your brothers. Choose who it shall be."

Yudhishthira looked at the still forms of his brothers and said, "Restore to me Nakula, Yaksha."

"Why Nakula?" asked the spirit. "Isn't Bhima, the strong one, most useful to you? Or Arjuna, the skilled warrior?"

Yudhishthira answered, "I would be unrighteous if I looked only to my own benefit and begged for Bhima's or Arjuna's life. They are my own full brothers on both sides. Of my mother's children, I at least live. Nakula is my stepmother's son. If Nakula and Sahadeva should both die, then my stepmother's bloodline would end. Therefore, spirit, it is just and right that Nakula's life should be restored rather than Bhima's or Arjuna's."

As Yudhishthira said this, there appeared before him none other than Yama, God of Justice and Death, Yudhishthira's heavenly father. Yama embraced the young king and told him how pleased he was with his noble conduct and wisdom. He then restored to life not just one of the brothers but all of them.

In February, an early spring in southern India brings about a great blossoming of flowers, their scents swelling in the evening breeze and drifting from flower to field to the open windows of every home. Lakshmi is delighted by this time of year—not just for the cool before the furnace of summer but for the way spring seems to bewitch the youths.

She watches the boys and girls enact silent dramas with their brief glances as they loiter after school. Oh, thinks the storyteller, they are so spring-struck it is no different than watching peacocks fan their feathers for the hens! It seems many have fallen victim to the arrows of Lord Kamadeva, the God of Love.

The pauranika has sent word out that she will recount Kamadeva's tale tonight, so when dusk blushes the western horizon, the villagers find her sitting cross-legged upon her rosewood peeta, a low wooden stool, in the temple. As everyone knows the storyteller's other needs for a long tale—a framed picture of Lord Ganesha, two tall oil lamps, and her harmonium—these items are quickly fetched and the lamps are lit and placed on either side of the picture while her listeners seat themselves.

Sliding the fingers of her right hand along the instrument's keys, the storyteller starts to pump its bellows with her left, releasing its soft, melodious voice. Soon, encircled by lamplight and an attentive, eager audience, she begins with a call and response hymn in order to honor and invoke the elephant god, Lord Ganesha, Lord of Success and Wisdom. Having done so, she can begin the story of Kamadeva, the god whose powers awaken the charms of spring and all its gifts.

Lord Kamadeva, God of Love

 Brahma, the magnificent Four-Faced God, surveyed his handiwork, the earth he had created. What he saw greatly pleased him in its perfection: The oceans and lakes fed the sky with clouds, and the clouds fed the earth with rain. The animals breathed in what the plants breathed out, and so too in reverse. Every creature served another, as did the vegetation—all had a role and a purpose. All were dependent on one another for survival.

Yet Brahma felt some potential lacking—his project was, perhaps, too… predictable. He longed for some surprise, something unexpected. Thus Brahma gave a smile to the heavenly assembly of his sons, the Seven Sages, and created a youth of such remarkable beauty that the sages gasped. The boy's form was perfect—a broad chest, sculpted limbs, and a face that shone serene as the moon. The youth held a large bow made of sugarcane, with a bowstring of humming bees. A quiver slung across his shoulder held five kinds of arrows, each tipped with a different flower: rose, jasmine, champak, lotus, and tuberose. A colorful green parrot, his mount, waited nearby for his bidding.

Upon his sudden arrival, the boy looked around in confusion and asked Brahma, "Why have I been created? Why am I here?"

Brahma replied, "You are to be the God of Love, empowered with all the tools of enchantment. Your luster will evoke the spell of moonlight upon all whether it is day or night, and your arrows will rouse longing in any being you choose."

The boy said, "How can I kindle love in others when I have not experienced it myself?"

"I will create a worthy mate for you, who will help you to fulfill this duty and destiny." Thus speaking, Lord Brahma meditated and created another beauty of beauties, the maiden Rati, and then introduced her to Kamadeva as his wife.

Then Kamadeva asked, "When can I test my powers of love?"

Answering perhaps too quickly, Brahma said, "Right now."

So before Brahma could think to stop him, the boy took the jasmine-tipped arrow from his quiver and shot Brahma. Then, before any of the assembly could flee, he shot them with the four other types of arrows. Immediately, they felt the stirrings of love and desire. Lord Shiva, who happened to be passing by, witnessed the whole spectacle, and rebuked Lord Brahma.

Brahma, snapping out of his love-stupor, felt deeply humiliated and turned his anger on Kamadeva. "Kamadeva, you have brought upon me great dishonor in front of Lord Shiva! May he burn you up so you may never again pierce me with your arrows of passion!"

"But it was you who asked me to test my powers!" said Kamadeva. "I only did as you wished."

Realizing that the youth had tried to be obedient, Brahma softened his curse a bit. In its stead, he decided to give Kamadeva the greatest of all challenges. He said, "Lord Shiva is mourning the death of his wife Sati on Mount Kailasa. He has vowed never to marry again, and to perform severe tapasya, deep and harsh meditations to mourn her forever. With all your weapons of enchantment, you will stir him from his meditation and fill his heart with love."

"But there must be an object for his desire!" objected Kamadeva.

"That will come in time," said Brahma, "Soon enough, a maiden will come to serve Lord Shiva and you will be able to complete your task and cast off the curse."

So Kamadeva and Rati embarked on their difficult journey, only to return a few years later, discouraged and distraught, saying, "We have never seen anyone so aloof! Does Lord Shiva possess a heart? While he sat meditating amidst the most terrible storms of the icy Himalayas, we placed warm blankets beside him. Shiva ignored them. We surrounded him with colorful gardens that we glazed with the moon's milky light every evening. We brought before him but-terflies twirling in the breeze, peacocks and hens dancing for each other, rose petals unfolding in the first light of dawn. We opened every blossom known until the air was perfumed thick as a cloud. He took no notice."

But Brahma sighed and scolded the couple for their impatience. He reassured Kamadeva and Rati that they would be successful when the time was right and asked them to continue their efforts.

At this point in our tale a new character appears, for as everyone knows, love is rarely a straight path. In fact, with the birth of this demon, an asura named Taraka, the story becomes very complicated. Like all great demons, Taraka's birth was heralded by all the most frighten-ing omens of the world: mobbing crows, howling jackals, and an eclipse of the sun. And like every demon, Taraka had only a single wish when he came of age—to be more powerful than anyone else in the world.

For one hundred years Taraka lived on nothing but the moisture of clouds; for another hundred years he balanced upside down upon a single finger; for another hundred years he lay splayed upon sharp stones in the burning sun. After a thousand years of such trials, such a glaring blaze of light shone from his forehead that the gods took notice and feared that he might well turn them to ash. Much like Lord Shiva, he had undertaken the difficult rigors of purification, until, through his diligence, he had acquired daunting powers.

Soon the gods became so terrified of the demon Taraka that they asked Indra, King of the Gods, to intervene on their behalf. Indra went straight away to Lord Brahma and begged him to stop the asura from these exercises that gained him more and more power and threatened all of heaven.

Approaching Taraka, Brahma did his very best to negotiate, offering many rewards, but the demon was as stubborn as he was strong. "Only under one condition will I stop," said Taraka. "Grant me complete invincibility and immortality."

Brahma shook his head no, saying that those kinds of promises lead to a lot of devilment and chaos. So Taraka changed his offer. "All right, then—I will give them up if I am made invulnerable to attack from everyone except one born from the marriage of the mighty Lord Shiva himself." Taraka, like all who inhabited the divine realms, knew that Kamadeva and Rati's mission to interest Shiva in romance had utterly failed. Thus the asura felt certain he would never be in danger.

Brahma, flustered, aware that Indra and all the other gods waited in desperation for him to stop the demon, decided to agree to Taraka's condition. "Yes," Lord Brahma said. "I grant you that boon."

Naturally, because power feeds on itself, in no time at all the evil Taraka had used his might to take over Bhoo Loka, the earthly realm, as well as the heavenly realm, Deva Loka. He tyrannized everyone, the strong and the weak. Taraka assaulted women and executed men for no reason other than that he could do so. He disgraced each of the gods by stealing their weapon or mount. From Indra, Taraka snatched his prized white elephant, Airavata. He stole the sun's chariot, causing a terrible confusion between night and day. The world had never encountered such a power as Taraka. Even when Vishnu, Sustainer of the Universe, tried to help by hurling his discus Sudarsana across the heavens to cut off Taraka's head, he found his weapon returning unsuccessful for the first time ever.

Still in grave danger, the gods approached Brahma again and implored him to destroy this terrible demon he had helped create. But Brahma replied, "I cannot destroy something to which I have granted invincibility."

Thus Vishnu and Brahma found themselves unable to fight Taraka's ruthless greed. All that remained was Lord Shiva, the third of the trinity, for Brahma's boon meant that Shiva's offspring alone could kill the demon Taraka. However, as Kamadeva and Rati had discovered, Shiva had foresworn pleasure as well as all interest in love and marriage.

How, the gods wondered, would they ever interest Shiva in romance so that his offspring could vanquish the evil Taraka? Kamadeva and Rati were summoned again to use their powers of enchantment. Begging for any other duty than this, they trembled in fright at the task at hand. To disturb Shiva from his meditation would arouse his swift temper and risk him setting them ablaze with his fearsome third eye. But the world's fate hung in the balance, so Kamadeva and Rati resigned themselves to duty and a journey back to the high slopes of Mount Kailasa, where Shiva resided.

Meanwhile, at exactly the same time as the gods' terrible crisis, a daughter was born to the wife of Himavan, the god of the great Himalaya Mountains, the tallest peaks in the world. All her life, the child's mother had prayed and prayed to Shakti, Mother Goddess of All. When her daughter, Parvati, was born, the babe revealed herself—only to her mother—as an incarnation of Shakti.

Despite being an embodiment of the most powerful female force, Parvati grew up like any youngster. Sometimes she amused herself with wildflowers and butterflies beside the mountain streams, and sometimes she ventured far from home with her father. But her favorite trips of all were to visit Mount Kailasa, home of Lord Shiva.

Shiva, fortifying his defenses against all worldly delights, forbade Himavan from bringing his daughter in the future. But Parvati, being none other than the female half of Shiva's spiritual power, begged and begged her father. She wanted nothing more than to be around this holy being. Relentlessly persistent, Parvati finally got her way and devoted herself to the sacred tasks of attending to the heavenly sanctuary.

No sooner had this arrangement been made than the gods saw a glimmer of hope, a chance for the destruction of Taraka and the restoration of peace and order in the universe. Lord Shiva would have an object for his love! Realizing that this was the time that Brahma had alluded to, Kamadeva and Rati readied themselves to finish their perilous task and work the charms of romance upon Shiva and Parvati.

As soon as they arrived at Mount Kailasa, they hid—Kamadeva in front of Rati. Kamadeva began to soften Shiva's heart by summoning an untimely spring that thawed the frozen wasteland. Shiva, sensing the sun's unusual warmth and smelling the first blossoms, opened his eyes from meditation. Surprised and looking about, he asked aloud, "Why is spring so early?"

Just then Kamadeva shot both Shiva and Parvati with two of the lotus-tipped arrows that bend the mind toward forgetfulness. Shiva opened his eyes and his heart began to fill with love for Parvati. He quickly shut his eyes and put the thought from his mind. Meanwhile Parvati, sweeping with her back to Lord Shiva, found a sudden smile upon her lips and a heart beating with love for him.

Kamadeva shot both Shiva and Parvati with four more shafts each, including the arrows tipped with the fragrant champak flower. When Shiva next opened his eyes, the world looked new and fresh. To Parvati, everything shone with sudden luster: Colors shimmered and the sky appeared a lapis blue. Parvati turned toward Shiva to speak but found herself completely shy and tongue-tied.

Shiva clamped his eyes shut and took stock of himself. How could this lovely maiden be the same girl who had attended to him so earnestly and for so long? Finding his heart bursting with love, Shiva suddenly realized that a profound change had come upon him. How could he stray so far from his discipline and austerities? Since nothing had changed in the situation between Parvati and himself, Shiva began to suspect foul play. "Who has dared to disturb my meditation?" he wondered angrily.

With his third eye, the mind's eye of insight, he saw that the culprit was Kamadeva, hiding behind a nearby bush. When Shiva opened his eyes this time, his third eye, capable of extinguishing the world in an instant, turned poor Kamadeva into a handful of ash. Witnessing this harrowing spectacle, Rati, Kamadeva's wife, came out from hiding and ran to the spot where her husband had vanished. She fainted in grief and fell to the ground.

Shiva then fled Mount Kailasa until he could regain his senses. Weeping, Rati gathered the ashes of her husband in her palms and returned to Deva Loka, heaven. Parvati stayed behind, bereft and lonely, but as dutiful as ever in attending to the sanctuary.

Eventually Shiva returned to Mount Kailasa, and so impressed was he with Parvati's loyalty and devotion that they married. A son was born of their love, the six-faced god Kartikeya, who, even as a youngster, soon fulfilled his destiny, waging a fierce battle against the evil Taraka and defeating him forevermore.

Rati, Kamadeva's widow, had waited for this joyous moment, and without further delay, rushed to Shiva and Parvati on Mount Kailasa. Opening the corner of her sari, she showed them the handful of ash she had tucked safely into it: all that was left of her husband, the Lord of Love. She begged Shiva to bring him back to life.

"He has only lost the physical body that we see," said Shiva. "Do not worry. He is still right there," he said, gesturing toward the ashes.

"But how can I be married to an invisible husband?" Rati wailed. "This will be no life for me! He was the most lovely immortal in all the world!"

Feeling for Rati and concerned about a world void of love and desire, the other gods rushed to Rati, surrounding her and intervening on her behalf. "Lord Shiva, if you have destroyed the god of love and desire, how will the world go on functioning? What other force will bring beings together?"

Shiva, filled with love himself now and thus not so stern as before, softened. "Very well, then," he said, and turned to Rati. "I grant that you will be able to see your husband in his full form and glory. But just you."

Lord Shiva then proclaimed to the assembled gods, "Although Kamadeva will be visible to his wife only, the couple's charms of allurement will persist for all time. They will continue to act upon the world with all their previous tools of enchantment: the five types of blossom-tipped arrows, spring and its warm breezes, a thousand birdsongs, and flowers bursting on every stem and tree. The moon will forever shine upon the joyful song and dance of love-filled hearts."

"So you see," says the pauranika as she ends her story, "the world is once again bewitched by the charms of Lord Kamadeva, who has sent us this early spring! And I wonder who will feel his blossom arrows this year?" Eyes smiling, she looks around at the faces of the young and old caught in the soft glow of her lamplight. "Yes, all is exactly as it should be. We are each ready for the arrival of spring and its gifts."

The Barking Dog

Once, long ago, there lived a king who cared for none but himself. He had grown richer and richer from the high taxes levied upon his kingdom, while his subjects became poorer and poorer. Although the king's table spilled over with sumptuous delights, his subjects ate one meager meal a day, and sometimes not even that. But the heartless king did not care. He had all he wanted—wealth and power. His subjects, desperate for food, prayed fervently to Lord Krishna for help.

One day Krishna, disguised as a hunter, came to the palace gate intending to teach the heartless king a lesson. He brought with him an enormous, white hunting dog. The king was fond of such pursuits, and this colossal dog fascinated him. The hunter and his dog were both welcomed into the palace grounds. Then, leaving the dog in the king's care, Krishna went for a rest.

But this dog was no ordinary dog. The first time he opened his mouth to bark, a thunderous noise shook the stone walls of the palace, frightening the king and all his courtiers. Worst

of all, it was soon apparent that the dog would not stop barking. Desperate, the king sent for the hunter.

"What's wrong with your dog?" the king demanded.

The hunter said, "The dog is hungry."

Immediately, the king ordered that a big plateful of meat be brought. The mammoth dog licked the plate clean, and began to bark again.

A second plateful of meat was brought. The dog gobbled it up and continued barking and barking and barking.

With the palace walls beginning to crumble and his finest dishes and goblets crashing to the floor with each shuddering bark, the king could stand no more. "Take your dog away and leave my kingdom immediately!" he commanded the hunter.

"Your Majesty, we came at the request of your subjects, who are starving and struggling," said Lord Krishna. "The dog is here to stay."

"Then what will make him stop barking?"

"There are some people in this kingdom who eat all the food and do not share it with those who grow it, Your Majesty." Krishna leveled his eyes at the king. "As a result, your subjects battle hunger. This special dog feels the hunger of every person who does not have enough food."

The king's eyes widened in disbelief.

"As long as even one soul is hungry," said Krishna, "this dog, too, will be hungry, and will bark and bark and bark."

Now the king looked both frightened and confused, and perhaps even a little desperate. It had never occurred to him that the happiness of others was as important as his own contentment. After all, he was king. Shouldn't his people simply serve and obey their king?

His thoughts quickly fell apart as the dog seemed to double its efforts at disturbing the peace, barking twice as fast and loud. The king clapped his hands over his ears, knowing he would soon go mad with the continuous barking. "Something must be done!" he said The king gathered his wisest advisors together to consider the best course of action. They did not hesitate to make a unanimous decision: Each and every person in the kingdom must be fed right away.

Accepting their judgment, the king began to shout, point, and command: "Put all the servants on the palace grounds to work at once! Go to the storerooms and get all the bags of rice you can find! Take all the meat from storage! Gather every last vegetable from my gardens and all the fruit from my orchards!"

When these orders were set in motion, the king paused, sighed, and at last began to reflect on his years of selfishness. Full of remorse, he spoke kindly to his staff for the first time: "Continue to give generously of these foods, and keep on giving food until not a single man, woman, or child in the land is hungry!"

Soon a line of carts, teetering with bags and baskets of food piled high, rolled out through the palace gates. All that day and the day after, and the day after that, the carts continued, until they had stopped at every village in the land and found every house where someone suffered from hunger.

At last the day came when the enormous dog stopped barking and lay down quietly beside the king's throne. With the dog by his side, the king never reverted to his old ways. Only twice did the dog bark to remind the king about justice, and each time the king quickly fixed the problem. Inside the palace walls as well as outside of them, the king and his subjects lived out their years in perfect peace.

Shankara and the Outcaste

 Once, many centuries ago, there lived a young and wise teacher named Shankara. Shankara was deeply devoted to Lord Shiva and Goddess Parvati and wrote many hymns in their praise that are still sung today. Shankara preached that God is One and that God is in everyone equally. He led the life of a simple ascetic and traveled all over India to share his teachings. Wherever he went, people would flock to hear him speak. Following the wandering sage, many became his devoted students.

One morning, Shankara and his disciples were returning after a bath in the Ganges River when they saw a dalit man with his four dogs approaching in a drunken manner from the opposite direction. Dalits were considered the lowest class in Hindu society and treated as outcastes or untouchables. They often performed what was considered the most foul work, such as butchering animals, cleaning toilets, working in cremation grounds, and hauling trash.

As the man drew closer, Shankara's disciples ran ahead, admonishing him to move aside until the great teacher passed. The dalit looked quite filthy—his body glistened with sweat, his hands and feet caked with mud, his clothes torn in places, his hair unkempt—and yet his face was radiant with a mysterious glow.

While Shankara was taking all this in, the man continued to advance, wobbling, swerving as if drunk, his pot of country liquor sloshing upon and staining his dhoti. Alarmed, Shankara shouted, "Hey, you! Get out of the way! We have just had our morning bath. Make way so we can pass."

Pretending not to hear, the man continued to lurch in his direction. "Are you deaf?" shouted Shankara. "Do you know who I am? I am Shankara, a renowned teacher. Now, get out of the way!"

At last, nearly face to face with the dalit, Shankara was forced to take a few steps backward so as not to get too close to the man, who reeked of alcohol. "This is outrageous!" Shankara fumed.

"Oh Great Teacher," said the man, "I am sorry if I offend you. I will gladly move out of the way if you can answer my questions."

Angered by the dalit, a student of Shankara said, "How dare you? You who are an out-caste have no right to question a great spiritual master!"

But the dalit would not budge.

Shankara intervened and said, "What are your questions? Ask quickly so I can answer and get on my way!"

"My first question," said the dalit, "is this: When I cut my hand, it bleeds red as a poppy's petals. Does yours not bleed thus?" He shoved his filthy hand in front of Shankara's face.

The teacher, of course, would have liked to swat it away, but then he quickly reconsidered —touching him would mean going back to the river for another bath and that would take a lot of time. He kept his hands to himself.

The dalit pressed on: "In what respect is your body different from my body? We share the same physical elements and our bodies perform the same functions!" Shankara said nothing.

"So tell me," the man continued, "is not the earth on which I am standing the same as the one on which you and your disciples are standing?"

Again, the teacher found no words to respond, so the dalit said, "I live beneath the vast canopy of the sky. So do you. The gentle breeze that's blowing is touching both of us. Does that make the air unclean? If so, that means that you, also, are unclean."

Thrusting his clay pot under the teacher's nose, the man demanded, "Is the sun reflected in the river different from the sun reflected in my drink?"

Completely flummoxed, Shankara could not respond to a single question.

"You asked me to move aside. To whom were your words addressed, O Wise One? To my body or my soul—my Atman? If it is my Atman, isn't it the same in all of us, divine and pure? You, Shankara, like to preach that we are all one in God. What then, truly, is the difference between us?"

Wordless and stupefied, the teacher lowered his eyes. Here was an uneducated outcaste able to summarize the very essence of Shankara's own teachings. At a loss for any logical explanation of the situation, the sage began to meditate. Eyes half-closed, he sensed more than saw the presence of the Divine. He recognized that none other than the god Shiva stood in disguise before him and understood that Lord Shiva himself had come in the form of a dalit to test whether Shankara understood and believed the truth of his own teachings.

Shankara fell at the feet of the dalit, saying, "He who has achieved the ability to see God everywhere is my guru, my teacher, be he an outcaste or a priest." Then Shankara burst into a hymn of praise to Lord Shiva.

Pleased with Shankara's devotion, Shiva revealed himself and said, "You are indeed a wise human, O Shankara, but needed to follow your own teachings. On your path to wisdom, you had yet to practice the most important lesson of all—to treat every human being equally, regardless of their social class. Each person deserves your utmost respect and compassion, your mercy and justice, as everyone has the same worth and divinity."

Thus speaking, Lord Shiva blessed Shankara and disappeared.

This August afternoon, Lakshmi rests on a small wooden bench in the shade behind her home. A slight breeze moves the air, tousling her sari around her ankles like flags of silk. It tickles a bit. A few cows low in the distance—she hopes that they, along with their cowherd, have secured some shade from the blazing heat.

"Lalitha," she calls out to her granddaughter playing in the yard. "Come help me polish Lord Ganesha, the Elephant-Headed God, for his upcoming festival, and I will tell you the wondrous story of his birth."

Barefoot, the eight-year-old girl races across the dirt, dashes into the house, and halts abruptly in front of the cupboard near the altar. Carefully, she lifts the brass statue from the cupboard and carries it in two hands to her grandmother, now sitting cross-legged on the back porch.

Ganesha is Lord of Success and Wisdom, watching over all the affairs in every Hindu home. Lalitha smiles every time she sees him. It's hard to be glum looking at his elephant head perched on a chubby child's body. Like every god, Ganesha has a loyal mount to ride upon, and even that mount, a fearless, quick, and clever mouse named Mushika, makes her laugh.

Lalitha plunks down next to her *nannamma*, her grandmother, and hands the statue to her. Lakshmi uses a special concoction made of tamarind pulp, ash, and lime juice for shining brass. "So," the pauranika says as she begins to rub the mouse under Ganesha's foot. "Here is the story I promised you of Ganesha's birth."

The Birth of Ganesha

 On the majestic peak Kailasa, within the great Himalayan mountain range, lived the god Shiva, his beautiful wife, the goddess Parvati, and thousands of his minions, called *ganas*. Without Shiva the Destroyer, the world could never renew itself—seasons would never change and life would come to a standstill. He wears a snake for a necklace, for the snake sheds its old skin for the new one it has ready, remaking itself many times over. In his matted hair he wears a moon, for the moon is like a clock in the sky, and Lord Shiva has power over time. He smears his body all over with grey ash, to remind us all that death is a certainty. We are each miracles created from the earth, and when we die, we are turned back into ash and dirt. By rubbing himself with ash, Shiva reminds us to make every moment of life count!

Living atop Kailasa, Lord Shiva loved the biting cold of the high altitudes, the snow, the frosty slopes, and the dense forests right below them. Draped in a tiger skin and serpent, he spent his days sitting cross-legged under a towering pine, meditating and listening to the prayers of his devotees the world over. Sometimes he would leave home to travel the earth on his giant bull, Nandi, to bestow blessings upon his followers. At other times, he was called to fight the forces of evil with the help of his ganas. On those occasions, his wife, the Goddess Parvati, would often be home alone for hundreds of years.

One day, Lord Shiva was called away on an urgent mission of this kind. Once again, Goddess Parvati was left behind. She could no longer stand the ache of loneliness. She decided to create a little child to keep her company.

Parvati proceeded to gather clay from the sacred mountain. She wet it, mixed it thoroughly, and molded it. As she worked, beads of her perspiration fell into the clay. Out of these elements, she fashioned a little boy, perfect in every detail. She decked him with gold ornaments and clothed him in beautiful clothes. "How handsome you are!" she said to the statue, gazing in admiration and joy at her own creation. "How strong and powerful you look!" So saying, Parvati took a deep breath and gently blew on the clay figure. The boy immediately came to life and stood before her smiling. Then he honored his mother by kneeling at her feet and bowing deeply.

The goddess blessed the boy in turn, saying, "You are a part of my sweat and breath, my son. I will always love you and care for you." When the boy called her Amma, Mother, Parvati hugged him and her heart sang with joy.

The young boy was strong as well as playful. He followed Parvati around all day long, keeping her amused and happy with his chatter and curious observations. For her part, Parvati taught her son to read and write and the many arts. Because of his heavenly qualities, when he sang or danced in the forest, he found that all the animals—mighty or meek—romped alongside.

Days and months went by. Although Parvati did not feel so alone anymore, she still longed to see her husband, who had yet to return. One morning, the very morning Shiva planned to return, Parvati said to her son, "My child, I am going to take a leisurely bath and don't want to be disturbed. Please stand guard at the door to my quarters and do not let anyone enter without my permission."

Delighted with this important task, the boy picked up a spear and stationed himself, determined to stop all who might dare to enter. Knitting his brows and squaring his jaw, he did his best to appear menacing. Like a sentry, he walked back and forth, back and forth in front of the closed door.

Not long after the boy took his post, Lord Shiva returned to the mountain. A fearsome sight, draped in tiger skin, Shiva strode through the front door of his home, followed by an icy wind. He proceeded toward his wife's room, where he saw a little boy guarding the entrance. Struck by the boy's handsome form and confidence, Shiva wondered who this child might be—he had never seen him before. Tired and hungry, however, he was too impatient to inquire. He longed for some rest and was eager to see his wife. But as he approached the door, to Shiva's astonishment, the boy barred his way.

"Halt!" the youngster said to Lord Shiva. "No one is allowed to enter without my amma's permission!"

Taken aback, Shiva said, "Your amma? Who are you, little boy? And how dare you talk to me like that? Do you know who I am? I am the almighty Shiva, Lord of the Universe, the Three-Eyed One, the one who has the ability to destroy and rebuild anything. Get out of my way before I slay you!"

"I don't care who you are or what you can do," said the fearless boy. "You still are not allowed to enter my amma's room!" So saying, the boy struck Shiva's hand with his spear.

"You fool!" Shiva shouted. "I am Lord Shiva, Parvati's husband. How dare you forbid me from entering my own home and seeing my wife!"

The young boy did not utter a word, but once again struck Shiva with his spear. As he was frequently wont to do, Shiva erupted in a rage. Losing all restraint, blind with anger, the god lifted his weapon and without hesitation cut off the child's head, sending it far off the mountain into space.

At that very moment, Parvati opened the door and saw her son lying lifeless on the floor.

"You have killed my son!" she screamed in horror.

"What? Who? Your son? But we have no son!" said Shiva.

Parvati cried in grief. "O Shiva, because we are one in body and spirit, two halves of a whole, that was our son, our very own child whom I created from clay and my sweat! How could you kill him?"

Through her tears she told Shiva the circumstances of the boy's birth. When Shiva heard the tale, he was stricken by remorse. "Oh, Parvati, what an awful and terrible thing I have done," he lamented. "My heart was wild with anger, and I killed our innocent and beautiful child."

But by then, Parvati's grief had turned to anger. "Go now!" she ordered Shiva furiously, "and do not return until you find his head and fix it to his body! Not only must my son regain his life, but he must be given the supreme place of honor among all gods for his bravery."

"I promise to do as you wish," said Shiva.

He dispatched all his *ganas*, his minions, to find the boy's head. Spreading out in all directions, combing all the forests of Mount Kailasa, they searched and searched but could not locate it. And so they returned empty-handed and dispirited.

Despairing, Shiva realized that they might run out of time to save the god-boy if they could not find his head. So Shiva himself decided to go to earth and return with the head of the first creature that crossed his path, human or animal.

As it happened, the first creature that he came across in the forest was an old elephant. The elephant bowed before Shiva and said, "O Lord of the Universe, what is it that causes you to be so sad?"

"I have committed a dreadful crime," said Shiva. "Thoughtless with fury, I have killed my own son. I cut off his head and now it is lost. If I don't replace it soon, he will never live again."

The elephant bent to its knees and placed its head on Shiva's feet, saying, "O Great One, I have lived a good and long life, and feel grateful for the many gifts and blessings that you bestowed upon me. Please take my head. It would be an honor to give my life so your son can live again."

Deeply moved by the elephant's words, Shiva placed his hands on the elephant's broad forehead, blessing him. "I thank you for your generous and selfless offer. May your soul be blessed with eternal life, and reside in the heavenly realms."

Shiva then cut off the elephant's head, raced back home with it, and fitted it atop the boy's body. Parvati laid her healing hands upon the boy and, once again, breathed life into him.

The boy opened his eyes, stretched sleepily, and smiled. Parvati hugged him and wept with joy.

"My son," Shiva said, "I made a terrible mistake, for which I am deeply sorry. Since you were such a valiant guard, I appoint you the leader of my ganas, and therefore, you will be called Ganesha. The head of a great elephant, his gift to you, will make you as wise as you are strong and brave." The elephant-boy's face shone with delight.

Shiva continued, "From this day onward, for eternity, you shall be worthy of worship. People will pray to you first, before they worship any other god, just as your mother has asked. You shall be the Remover of Obstacles, the God of New Beginnings, Lord of Success and Wisdom."

The pauranika ends the birth story of Ganesha and adds one more thing. "I bet you already know, Lalitha, that the selfless act of the old elephant for the god is why many temples safeguard elephants."

"I do, Nannamma," says Lalitha.

"So gaze upon the shiny Lord Ganesha!" She holds the statue in the flat of her palm. "What do you think? Have I cleaned and polished him well? Is he as gold as the sun now?" She moves to stand. "Give me your hand and help your old grandmother up. Let's put Ganesha back on the altar with a food offering; he will remain there until the coming festival. And then, perhaps, we should pay a visit to the village temple and honor the elephant there? Maybe she, too, would like something to eat?"

The Wise Girl

Once upon a time there lived two old teachers in a hermitage in the forest. They spent most of their days meditating and praying to Vayu, God of Wind. One day, having spent all morning chanting prayers and performing various rituals in praise of Vayu, the sages readied themselves for their noon meal as usual. They were famished and eager to eat.

However, just as the sages began their lunch, a young student arrived at the doorstep with a begging bowl in her hands.

"Dear Sirs," the girl said, bowing before them, "can you please spare some of your food? I am really hungry!"

"No, I'm sorry," replied one of the sages at once. "We cannot share any of it with you. This food was specially prepared for us as a reward for our constant devotion to our god."

Undiscouraged, the girl then asked, "O Great Teachers, could you tell me which god you worship?"

"We worship mighty Vayu, God of Wind. He is also known as Prana, Breath of Life."

The girl responded, "Then you must know, Learned Sirs, that Prana permeates everything in the universe—Prana is all that moves. Prana is spirit—that which animates all creation."

"Yes, yes, we know all that," the sages replied impatiently. Their food was getting cold.

"Respected Sirs, before you started to eat, to whom did you make the offering of food?" asked the girl.

"Who else but Prana?"

The girl waited in silence. "Young lady, what exactly are you trying to tell us?" one of the men asked angrily.

"Forgive me for delaying your delicious feast, Venerable Ones," she said. "If Prana pervades everything, it pervades me too. I am but a part of the universe, am I not?"

At this remark both men began to feel ashamed. They fixed their gaze elsewhere than the girl. After a time one stammered, "Yes, you are."

"Isn't it Prana that lives in this hungry body that stands before you and speaks?" the girl asked.

"Yes, it is," they responded in unison, at last understanding her point.

"Well then, O Revered Ones, by denying me food, aren't you denying Prana, the very god for whom you prepared the food?"

The two sages, who till then had only grasped the surface meaning of their daily rituals and prayers, realized the truth behind the girl's words. They apologized to the young girl for their selfishness, invited her to join them, and thanked Lord Vayu for bestowing the blessings of both food and wisdom upon them.

The pauranika stands in her doorway. After sunset, the deafening chorus of crickets in the trees surrenders to the solo claims of bullfrogs in their rice paddy kingdoms. A faithful evening breeze greets her.

Looking up, she sees a three-quarter moon and guesses it will set by midnight. In her heart, she hopes that the nights here will never be ruined by pollution. City dwellers rarely look up, and if they do, she thinks, the glory of the night sky hides behind a smoggy blanket. Nothing, thinks Lakshmi, sparks her imagination—and her audience's—like the brightness of the moon and stars of the countryside.

After a time, the storyteller walks back into her home and opens her clothes cupboard to pick out a sari for tonight's story—perhaps a light gold one, she muses, to mirror the moon. She takes a deep breath. She always has a story in mind, but sometimes someone voices a question that a different story will answer best. Not knowing exactly which story she'll end up telling, or where its side trips will take her audience, keeps her full of anticipation.

Of course, it is the children she hears arriving first—carrying their excitement with them like the wind, signaling the arrival of the rest of the village soon after. When Lakshmi steps outside, she sees that families have already assembled in front of her house. Mothers, patting their infants' backs, lower themselves onto palm mats to listen. The men stand toward the back, softly talking of coconut yields and prices.

The little ones race through the crowd as if it didn't exist, but when they see Lakshmi, they stop mid-stride while a place is cleared for her to sit. She takes a few moments to settle herself cross-legged with her harmonium on the porch, then begins to chant a prayer, a *sloka*, in praise of Lord Ganesha, Lord of New Beginnings and Wisdom. Her audience soon follows, repeating the words many times:

Vakratunda Mahakaya,
Suryakoti Samaprabha,
Nirvighnam Kuru Me Deva,
Sarva Karyeshu Sarvada.
Om shanti, shanti, shanti.

O Lord Ganesha, of curved trunk and massive body,
the one whose splendor is equal to a million suns,
please bless me so that
I do not face any obstacles in my endeavors.
Peace, peace, and perfect peace.

When Lakshmi lowers her voice to a whisper, so do the villagers, until the silence feels immense enough that everyone can almost hear the Moon God, Chandra, in his chariot arcing overhead.

Chaitra and Maitra

Once, not very long ago, a teacher had two very devoted students, Chaitra and Maitra. They couldn't have been more different from one another. Maitra, strong and able-bodied, quick and ambitious, tried to anticipate his teacher's every wish and be the first to fulfill it, elbowing Chaitra away from the guru whenever he could. Chaitra, for his part, was thoughtful and contemplative in nature and never acted impulsively. Perhaps some would call him lazy or slow because of the time it took him to consider things—certainly Maitra thought he was, and tried his best to convince the teacher so.

Because of Maitra's competitiveness, life with the two boys was always faintly unpleasant, like a small thorn that could not be removed. No matter the words of wisdom the teacher said to him, Maitra, running about, vigilant and determined to be the guru's favorite, seemed to miss the point.

One day their teacher decided he'd had enough. If words couldn't reach Maitra, perhaps action would. He concocted a lesson that would put the boys to a test. He gave them each a single rupee and took them to two empty rooms. "With this humble coin," said the guru, "you must fill your room."

Chaitra stood there, his interest piqued, and thought over the challenge, but Maitra took off at a run for the village bazaar to see if he could be the first to succeed. Of course Maitra soon discovered he could buy next to nothing with a single rupee. But another idea struck him, so feeling very clever indeed, he ran to the garbage seller and asked for a cart full of rubbish to take back to his room. The garbage seller, puzzled by the young man's agitation but delighted to be paid for the stinking pile, agreed and happily drove the cart to their home, with Maitra giving directions.

Arriving at their destination, they encountered Chaitra just leaving for the market. He smiled kindly at Maitra, held the single rupee up, and continued on his way. Maitra guffawed—too bad for Chaitra! He was just too slow—perhaps now their teacher would recognize that the boy had no zeal.

Delighted with himself, Maitra unloaded the cart and easily filled the room from floor to ceiling with ruined baskets, worn shoes, slimy banana peels, and rotten vegetables. Standing in the doorway, surveying the lot, he swelled a bit with pride--all this in less than an hour! No doubt the guru would show up soon and praise his accomplishment. However, the guru didn't seem to be around, and it was too stinky to stay in his room, so Maitra basked outside in the sunshine and his self-admiration, knowing his task complete.

All the time Maitra had been gone, Chaitra had sat in his room and meditated on the challenge. His mind having become quiet, the solution came to him just before Maitra's return. Chaitra walked to the village market, where he found an old man selling the three things he sought—a matchbox, an incense stick, and an oil lamp. Unhurried, he returned to his room, where he lit the sandalwood incense and then the lamp. A warm glow and a lovely scent suffused the whole room. Chaitra then sat down again to meditate.

Meanwhile, Maitra's impatience made it impossible for him to be still. He paced about, mumbling and angry. Where was the teacher? If he didn't arrive soon, how would he ever know Maitra succeeded first? Weren't cleverness and quickness the qualities his teacher sought in students?

A few hours later, when the guru ambled back to inspect the rooms, he turned on his heels without even entering Maitra's room—it reeked too much. He shook his head in disbelief, chuckled, and walked over to Chaitra's room, Maitra following on his heels.

Chaitra's room, softly illuminated, was filled with the fragrances of sandalwood and jasmine. The teacher stepped inside and encouraged Maitra to come too. Sitting in contemplation, Chaitra opened his eyes when he heard them.

"If I told you these rooms represented the contents of your mind and heart," the teacher said to both the boys, "which would you rather spend time in?"

Chaitra said nothing.

Maitra cast his eyes down. The answer was obvious.

"It takes so very little to be content," continued the teacher. "But if we run about, acting before thinking, in no time we may end up with a full mind, yes, but it will likely be stuffed full with garbage."

Indra and the Ants

Long, long ago, a most powerful demon in the guise of a sinister serpent began to swallow all the rivers of the earth. As a limbless snake formed of clouds, he wound around the jagged peaks and gaping valleys of the Himalayas, amassing—but never releasing—the waters of the world.

Desperate with thirst, animals and plants cried out in their various ways for help from the gods, yet even the gods felt powerless as they watched their palaces crumble to dust. The waters of life—the streams, the sap of plants and trees, and the blood coursing through our veins—belong to all, but the serpent watched with glee as the creatures below withered and perished.

It was Indra finally, King of the Gods, who reached far into the hideous coils of cloud, the serpent's body, with his thunderbolt—the weapon specially made for this purpose—to end the snake's dominion of drought. Immediately upon the monster's death, the waters trapped in its belly burst free, and their sweet music sang afresh through every rill, river, and creature of the earth's body.

With the world made right again, the demons, asuras, returned to their realm, Asura Loka, and the gods rose up to their heavenly realm, Deva Loka. Indra, now proclaimed their savior, puffed up with pride and vowed to undertake the rebuilding of every god's glorious mansion.

But first he set out to rebuild his own palace.

Summoning Vishvakarman, Architect of the Heavens, Indra commanded him to create an abode befitting the king of gods. And so, within a single year, Vishvakarman had erected just such a residence: marble floors inlaid with jewels and gold, columns and towers of glass between floors, dozens of wood balconies carved fine as lace. The Craftsman Lord built a hundred fountains casting the rainbows known as Indra's bow, and dug many serene lakes ringed by gardens and groves of fruit.

Yet whenever Indra surveyed the royal residence, he never felt satisfied. He could always envision more—perhaps ten more palace rooms, ten more pleasure grounds, and certainly more gardens, as well as coconut, banana, and mango groves. Lord Indra's wants and demands never ended. Vishvakarman, Lord of Crafts, found Indra impossible to please.

After some time of these ever-mounting demands, the master craftsman fell into despair. When Indra would still not listen to his entreaties to stop, Vishvakarman at last sought help from the god Brahma, the four-faced creator. He fell at Brahma's feet and appealed, "My Lord, Indra and I are both immortal; there will be no end to these ideas of his. I am caught in this for eternity, for there is no satisfying Indra's desires!" Brahma, who dwelled above the minor gods—above their ambitions, troubles, and discord—assured the craftsman that Indra's ceaseless demands would soon end.

Wanting absolute assurance that the problem would be solved, Brahma brought Vishvakarman's request to Lord Vishnu, Sustainer of the Universe. All-knowing, Vishnu saw that his

avatar, Krishna, would soon take care of the problem. With a slight nod to Brahma, Vishvakarman's request was granted.

The following morning, Krishna, disguised as a beautifu boy, arrived at the gates of Indra's vast palace. Followed by a crowd of enthralled children, the boy requested a meeting with Lord Indra. Because the boy held the staff of a religious pilgrim, the palace guard knew that this request could not be refused.

The gatekeeper hurried to his master, Lord Indra, whose duty it was to honor all such holy pilgrims. Indra hastened to his visitor at the gate, bestowed a blessing upon him, and invited the boy to the great hall, where he was welcomed with the traditional offerings of honey, milk, and fruit.

Indra studied the boy closely while he ate, noticing a radiance in the boy's face and a brilliance in his eyes. But Krishna, avatar of Vishnu, did not disclose his identity. In time Lord Indra asked, "Venerable young man, tell me why did you come here?"

"O King of Gods, I came to see this palace which I've heard so much about. I am told it is a palace unlike any built by the Indras before you! How long might the master craftsman Vishvakarman be busy with duties on your behalf?"

A fatherly smile at the boy's wild imagination crept across the god's face. He leaned toward the boy. "Indras before me? What are you talking about? I alone am Indra, King of the Gods. Tell me, young man, about these other 'Indras.' Have you met others?"

"Oh yes, many!" The boy's voice and presence, as sweet and soothing as honey, kept the god's anger at bay. "I even know your father, Kashyapa, the son of Brahma. I also know Lord Brahma, brought forth from the lotus in Vishnu's navel, as well as Vishnu himself, the Supreme Being."

Naturally, Indra did not believe the boy, but something marvelous in the boy's presence made him hold his tongue. Still, the god felt a chill of truth run through his body when he considered the boy's words—could it be possible that there were other Indras before him? Was he not the one and only King of Gods for all time?

Meanwhile, as boy and god conversed, an army of ants, four yards deep and four yards wide, made their way across the palace floor toward Indra's throne. Seeing this, the boy broke out in sudden laughter, but then, just as abruptly, fell silent.

Indra, truly puzzled, looked at the ants and then at the boy. "Why did you just laugh? And why are you sullen now?"

At first the boy would not answer, stating that the truth would hurt Indra. When Indra reassured the boy that he would not take offense, the boy said, "O King, if I told you the reasons for my laughter, you would understand both the world's greatest woe and its greatest wisdom at once. It would deal a death blow to your pride, desires, and ambitions as surely as an axe fells a tree."

"But you must," pleaded the god. "You must tell the King of the Gods such things! Tell me the key that will dispel the darkness of all ignorance." Despite the boy's warning, Indra felt irresistibly drawn to the knowledge.

At last the boy spoke. "O Indra! This army of ants marching toward you like soldiers is nothing other than a multitude of former Indras just like you! Each started as the smallest of creatures and, over time, through many good deeds, each ascended to your rank as King of Gods. Then believing that they were the most powerful and best of gods, they used their thunderbolt in reckless violence! Down, down they went, back to the beginning of Samsara— their cycle of lives—as ants again."

The boy looked over at the ants, which were now splitting into two streams around the god's throne. "But each, you can be sure, will ascend to King of Gods again," said the boy.

At this claim, Lord Indra guffawed. "How can this be so?" said Indra. "You yourself said no god had ever undertaken a project of such magnitude as mine."

"O poor King," said the boy, "this universe comes into being and then dissolves, only to be created afresh again countless times. Who can count the universes that exist side by side in different planes, each with their own Brahma and Indra? Of course there have been many Indras!"

The holy boy's gaze swept across Indra's great hall, landing here and there on gold filigree or on a mosaic of emeralds and rubies. The god followed the boy's eyes. Said the boy to the king, "The wise know this life to be finite, and but one of many. With this knowledge in their hearts, they neither boast of their accomplishments nor hoard their possessions. They are easily content and frugal in their ways."

At this, Lord Indra felt a terrible shrinking of his own importance, as if he were seeing himself from the great perspective of the future, feeble on his throne, old, not so mighty after all, and his new palace already on its way to disintegration.

Reading the god's mind, the boy said, "In unending cycles, all universes that are created will be destroyed. Creation and destruction will alternate, just as god and ant will change places."

As Lord Indra pondered these words and their significance, the holy boy, who was in reality an avatar of Vishnu, vanished as mysteriously as he'd arrived.

Moments later, Indra, greatly chastened and yet filled with wonderment, lost all desire to enlarge his projects further. Summoning the Lord of Arts and Crafts, Vishvakarman, to his side, Indra heaped treasures and thanks upon him and, at long last, released him to help others.

The Wise Minister

A long time ago in India, there lived a certain king who was full of good intentions and concern for his subjects. They, in turn, cared for him. But the king also tended to be impulsive and shortsighted, and as everyone knows, this can lead to a lot of problems. Luckily, the king had a very wise minister who kept a close eye on his highness, giving him good advice and counsel.

Once, during the wintertime, the king, his minister, and some of his courtiers went for a stroll in the royal garden. It wasn't so much a garden as a large park—from the palace tower one could not see from one end to the other. And even in the coldest months of the year, the grounds had plenty to admire, for nature unveils a simple and stark beauty in wintertime.

The royal retinue ambled down one path after another and finally chose to rest near a lake some distance from the palace. Wanting to feel refreshed, the king decided he'd like nothing more than to bathe his tired feet in the cool lake. A manservant dashed forward and removed his shoes. Another servant laid a satin cloth over the ground to protect the king from sharp rocks on his way to the water. When he reached the waterline, the king dipped his big toe in and instantly jumped backward; this lake, where he swam in the summer, felt much colder in winter than he had imagined! He wondered whether to proceed. And then one of his not-so-good ideas struck him: Was anyone in his kingdom tough enough to brave this lake?

He immediately announced to his courtiers, "I will give a reward of one thousand gold coins to anyone who can stand in this water up to their necks for a single night."

Concerned by the king's thoughtlessness, the wise minister whispered in the royal ear, "Your Highness, I don't think it's a good idea at all. No one will survive a whole night of standing in this water!"

But as so often happens with the powerful, once they've made a pronouncement, even a very bad one, the fear of being mocked for a change of heart made the king stubborn. Despite his minister's pleas, the king would not back down. As soon as the royal party returned to the palace, the challenge was announced across the kingdom to his subjects.

With such a large reward, the most eager and the first in line were the poor. They gathered by the lakeside and, one after another, stepped bravely into the water but scrambled back to shore when the water reached their knees. Finally, the poorest of them all came forward: a farmer whose crops had failed that year and who was left with neither rice nor lentils to feed his large family. Intent upon winning the king's prize, he strode into the lake until the water covered his shoulders. Determined, he spent the whole night standing without complaint. The next morning, the guards took the shivering man to the king to collect his rightful reward.

Surprised and delighted at this accomplishment, the king asked the farmer how he managed to survive the cold for so long. The farmer replied, "Your Majesty, by looking at the palace lights, I managed not to think of the cold. Seeing them reminded me of warmth and gave me courage."

Angered by this response, the king said, "You don't deserve the reward! You derived warmth from the palace lights. You cheated!" So saying, he sent the poor farmer away empty-handed. The wise minister tried to intervene on the farmer's behalf, but once again, there was nothing he could say to alter the king's course. So he decided to teach the king a lesson in another way.

A few days later, the minister invited the king and a few of his courtiers to dinner. The king arrived at the appointed time with his royal entourage in tow. The minister received them at the door and invited them to sit on cushions while the meal preparations were finalized. He let them know that the chefs were cooking the king's very favorite dish—lamb biryani, a savory rice dish of vegetables, a dozen spices, and meat. The king was delighted to hear this, and the men lounged about, expecting the delicious food to be served any minute.

But the biryani did not arrive. Instead, a few hours passed. The king began to feel hungry and irritable, so the minister went into the kitchen to check on dinner. He emerged from the kitchen and shrugged his shoulders apologetically, saying, "I am so sorry, Your Majesty, but the biryani is taking a long time to cook. It should be ready in just a few more minutes."

Another hour went by, and still no sign of food. By now the king was feeling really hungry and angry. He demanded to see for himself. When the king and his courtiers entered the kitchen, an amazing sight greeted them. A large copper pot hung from the ceiling, and far below it, resting on the floor, was a small oil lamp.

The king looked at the pot, then at the tiny flame, and then said to the minister, "What's this?"

The minister replied, "The lamb biryani, Your Majesty. As you can see, it's still being cooked."

"What nonsense!" yelled the king. "How can the heat from a small lamp reach a pot that's hanging so high?"

"Why not, Your Majesty?" replied the minister calmly. "If a poor man can warm himself by just looking at the palace lights from a great distance, then a pot can surely receive warmth from a lamp burning merely a few feet away!"

The king's face fell and his anger vanished as he understood his mistake. The next morning, the king called for the poor man whom he'd cheated and gave him twice the promised reward.

Enjoying a cup of spicy-sweet chai, Indian tea, on her porch bench one evening, the pauranika notices a group of about a dozen children walking her way. Kicking up the dust on the road as they approach in the waning light, they seem to be bickering about something. A boy jabs the air with his pointing finger and the group stops momentarily to consider his point, but then all begin speaking at once in response. They continue to head her way. Soon they gather at the end of the short path leading to the porch where she is sitting.

"Namaste, Grandmother," a girl says, pressing her two palms together and bowing her head slightly. Lakshmi smiles, acknowledging the greeting, and so the girl continues. "We have an issue we need you to settle between the boys and girls. These boys," and she gestures with her head in their direction, "do not believe that a goddess once proved herself better able than any male god to defeat evil in the universe. They say male gods are always more powerful."

The pauranika chuckles and says, "I believe it's possible that you are both right! To know the truth, we should revisit the story of Goddess Durga, for surely it is she of whom you speak!" She waves an arm to invite them nearer. "Perhaps you would all like to come sit on my porch, and I will recount the tale? Your timing is perfect, as I was just relaxing, looking at the clear sky, thinking about such things as men and women. Look!" she laughs, and they follow her gaze upward. "Even the sun and the moon, who accompany each other round and round for our entire lives, are paired in the sky today."

The youths seat themselves on outspread palm mats. The storyteller steps inside briefly and brings out a few items. "I just happened to have a nice picture of the Buffalo Slayer, Goddess Durga, here in preparation for her autumn festival," she says, showing them a painting of the goddess with many arms, each holding a different weapon as she dances within a ring of fire upon the fearsome buffalo demon Mahisha. Lakshmi leans the picture on the wall nearby and prepares to begin the story.

The Story of Goddess Durga

 The tale of Goddess Durga begins with the birth of an asura, a demon, called Mahisha. He was half buffalo and half man: hairy, very strong, and a terrible bully. Like all his demon brothers, he cared only about himself, and he never remembered that his selfishness always sowed the seeds of his own destruction. Unlike humans, asuras do not learn from their mistakes.

Soon after his birth, Mahisha came up with the same idea that every asura before him had had: He wanted to be the most powerful being in the universe. He wanted to rule the Three Worlds—the realm of the gods, the earth realm, and the realm of the asuras.

Most of all, Mahisha desired immortality. So in order to get the attention of his favorite deity, Lord Brahma, he began a strict regimen of severe tapasya, deep meditations, for ten thousand years. First he sat on a column forty feet tall for forty years to demonstrate his determination. Then, to show his strength and constancy, he pushed a mountain forward a handspan every day for two hundred years with his great horns and consumed nothing but air the whole time. Year after year, through his unflinching resolve, Mahisha's power and strength surged.

Impressed with such single-mindedness, Lord Brahma appeared before him. "I am pleased with your devotion, my son. What boon, what reward, do you seek?" said Lord Brahma.

Mahisha answered, "O Great Creator, I wish to have no fear of death. Please grant me the boon of immortality."

Each of Brahma's four faces looked just a little bit bored. He had heard this same request from every demon, but this did not stop them from trying yet again.

Brahma said, "Oh, Mahisha, all who are born must die one day; this is the eternal law of nature. I cannot grant immortality to any being! No, you cannot escape death. Ask any boon other than immortality and I will grant it."

Mahisha thought for a while and ventured, "O Grand Sir, grant then that no male—god, human, or asura—may cause my death. If I must die someday, my lord, let it be at the hands of a woman." Since Mahisha regarded it as impossible for a woman to attack and conquer him, he thought that he could trick Brahma into granting him immortality this way.

"So be it," said Lord Brahma, and he returned to his peaceful rest in the lotus of Lord Vishnu's navel.

A jubilant Mahisha, filled with pride and fervor on receiving his boon, returned to his kingdom to prepare for his conquest of the Three Worlds. He first conquered earth, Bhoo Loka. The many powerful kings who once ruled earth quickly found themselves his slaves, forced to pay tribute. Then Mahisha, drunk with power and new territory, decided to conquer heaven, Deva Loka, the abode of the gods. He sent a messenger to Indra, the King of the Gods, saying, "O Indra, abandon Deva Loka and go anywhere you like. Or choose to stay and serve me. I am the Supreme Lord of all. Either serve me, abandon your place, or if you are foolish enough, battle me."

Indra, upon hearing the message, sent his spies to determine the strength of Mahisha's army. Discovering that Mahisha had indeed amassed a huge and fearsome army, he met with his advisors and the minor gods to decide whether to go to battle. Since they were all uncertain, they went to Lord Brahma and sought his counsel. But Brahma, not one for conflict, advised them to visit Lord Shiva at his abode, Mount Kailasa. Shiva also sent them elsewhere, advising them to call on Lord Vishnu. Finally, after hearing all about the matter, Lord Vishnu proclaimed, "We will fight and vanquish this grass-eating demon."

The decision to go to war finally made, the gods traveled back to Deva Loka to await Mahisha. As soon as they arrived, however, Mahisha and his vast army launched a surprise attack.

Indra, Golden King of Heaven, was the first to confront the buffalo demon. Rushing forth with his thunderbolt in one hand and his bow in the other, he said, "Turn back, foolish Mahisha! Many asuras have tried to capture this place but failed. Why even try?"

"Because none before me possessed my strength or will!" said Mahisha. "Step aside, you spoiled ninny! Hand over all that is yours, and I may spare your life!"

Indra flushed with righteous anger and took another step toward the demon. "You are nothing but a dung-dropping buffalo in love with yourself. Your type has no place in Heaven. Now begone, or I will command my armies to vanquish every last one of your devil soldiers!"

"Indra, I've come to fight, not chat," said Mahisha, moving closer to the god. "If you are so very brave, use your weapons instead of your tongue!"

Unable to resist Mahisha's taunts any longer, Indra brandished his thunderbolt, ordered his army of gods and devas to attack the asura hordes, and charged at Mahisha himself.

A terrible battle ensued between the devas and the evil asuras. Because greed and desire multiply without end, Mahisha, the great beast of greed, created a million Mahishas in the sky as well as on the ground, each armed with a fearsome weapon. The devas, unsure of where or what to strike, began to lose confidence and flee.

Witnessing this dire situation, Indra pleaded with Brahma, Vishnu, and Shiva to join the battle. The Trinity entered the battle astride their giant mounts: Brahma upon his snow-white swan, Vishnu on his soaring eagle, and Shiva riding his magnificent bull.

Vishnu entered the war first, sending Sudarsana, his discus of ever-turning time, spinning into the battlefield. In a single stroke, it destroyed all of Mahisha's illusions. The demon stumbled in confusion but recovered all too quickly. The enraged Mahisha then attacked Vishnu with a weapon rarely seen before in the heavens, injuring the god so that he fell into a faint. Seeing Vishnu struck unconscious, Lord Shiva, God of Annihilation, entered the fray and attacked Mahisha with the full force of his trident. Mahisha deflected the blow with his mace, and then, with a second mighty swing, slammed the mace into Shiva's chest, knocking him down.

Never one to fight, Brahma, Grandfather of the Worlds, who carries only his scepter, book of wisdom, and prayer beads, looked on with dismay. With Vishnu and Shiva injured and taken to their abodes, Brahma realized that Mahisha was invulnerable and also withdrew.

Mahisha wasted no time in reaping the rewards of victory. He and his army routed the remaining gods, who fled to the forests and hills to hide in treetops and caves. Those gods and devas the demons captured were forced into slavery. "I am the true ruler of heaven," he said to his commanders and army. "From now on, I alone shall be worshipped."

Mahisha and his hordes then began to harass and torment those they suspected of continuing to worship Brahma, Vishnu, or Shiva. If they saw a holy offering of honey or flowers tucked behind a boulder, they searched until the culprit was discovered. Living in perpetual fear, devoid of joy or hope, the gods and their royal attendants sank into despair.

Driven from their celestial abodes and tired of wandering, Indra and several gods once again went to appeal to Lord Brahma to find a solution. They pleaded, "O Creator, we cannot live in hiding and in fear for eternity! The Three Worlds have collapsed into despair because of Mahisha's ruthless and terrible reign. Please do something!"

Indra and the devas then related in detail how Mahisha had continued to wreak havoc in heaven. "He flung me like a puppet from my throne," said Indra. Surya, the sun god, complained, "I can no longer travel around the world in my golden chariot, for Mahisha has snatched it away!" And a deva reported, "Agni, God of Fire, the messenger between heaven and earth, cowers in the back of a cave, blowing on one small ember!"

Brahma listened closely, nodding, uttering an occasional sympathetic "um" and "oh." "Yes, these demons always create mischief, don't they?" he said. "I propose that we discuss this again with Lord Shiva."

Off they went to Mount Kailasa where Brahma explained to Shiva that the demon Mahisha had driven the devas to wander all over, with no home of their own. Said Brahma, "Considering the dire circumstances, we have come to you."

Lord Shiva, shaking his head from side to side in exasperation, said, "Dear Brahma, you caused this mayhem by granting Mahisha's request that only a woman should be able to kill him! The asura has become so powerful that he was able to defeat us all in battle. Where would we find a woman so mighty? What woman can take on the evil one?"

Brahma said, "Although my wife, Saraswati, attends to learning and the arts, she's not very learned in the arts of war."

Shiva speculated, "Parvati, my wife, is courageous, but I worry she won't have the strength to defeat the demon on her own. So let us go to Lord Vishnu and ask him for a solution to this problem."

The devas entreated Lord Vishnu, but Vishnu soon interrupted them, saying, "Oh, this is an ancient, familiar tale. Every demon granted special powers becomes arrogant, promotes evil, and delights in tormenting gods and people alike. While they may succeed in the short term, don't worry. They will be overcome sooner or later."

Shiva said, "Still, as we failed in our first attempt to rout Mahisha with the best of our weapons, we should come up with a new plan, for perhaps the world teeters at the brink, as Indra says."

"Mahisha's demise must be wrought by a woman," said Indra.

Said Vishnu, "We need to pray to the Source from whom we are all derived: Shakti, the Great Goddess, Mother of All. With our spouses, let us pray to that fiery energy to come forth from all of us and manifest as a noble woman."

No sooner had Lord Vishnu offered the suggestion and the gods agreed than a great radiance emanated from their bodies and united into a blazing mountain, pervading all the regions of the sky with fire and light. A form slowly took shape, as Goddess Durga was born:

her head from the energy of Shiva; her many arms from the energy of Vishnu; her two feet from Brahma; her hair from the Lord of Death, Yama; her hips from the earth; her toes from the sun; and her ears from the roaring wind.

Awestruck by Durga's beauty and ferocity, the gods instantly recognized that she was more powerful and dangerous than any individual god or demon. The blaze of her creation was not their own but the splendor of the Great Divine Mother of All, Shakti. Her presence, fragmented among the gods and creatures of the Three Worlds, was at last reunited at its source.

The gods could not bear to look at directly at Durga. They knelt and together chanted, "O Durga, we bow to you! You are the source of all strength, the remover of all difficulties, the reliever of all suffering, the embodiment of perfection and power, the vanquisher of evil, and the restorer of peace. We bow to you, we bow to you!"

Then one by one, the gods approached her and laid their best weapons at her feet: Shiva, his trident; Vishnu, his discus; Brahma, his sacred kamandalu, a container filled with holy water; and Indra, his thunderbolt. Other gods offered yet more weapons, garments, and ornaments beyond compare, so that soon Durga was clothed as the queen of queens, and in each of her eighteen arms she held a terrifying weapon.

Finally, Himavan, the Lord of the Himalaya Mountains, came forward with a mighty lion for her to ride upon. "This lion," he said, "represents Dharma—righteousness, truth, and justice—and on his back you will regain the world." And the great gods and devas together shouted, "Hail to Goddess Durga, Restorer of Justice, she who will be called upon in all battles for victory."

Durga assured them, "O Gods, fear no more. I will seek out and destroy the evil Mahisha!" When she spoke thus, her voice reverberated through time and space, making the earth quake and mountains heave!

All this commotion reached the ears of Mahisha, and his heart skipped a beat. He bellowed and commanded all the asuras to prepare for war. In a storm of weapons, they quickly rallied around him. Surrounded by his mighty army, Mahisha rushed out of his palace to the source of the uproar, where he witnessed the most spectacular and menacing scene.

There stood Goddess Durga, radiant and resplendent, beautiful and ferocious, holding a multitude of weapons and seated majestically upon a lion. Her many arms stretched from horizon to horizon. The earth buckled under her feet. Her crown pierced the sky, and her defiant laughter reached the stars. The vision sent terror up Mahisha's spine.

Mustering courage, Mahisha said, "O Beautiful One, who are you? And why are you here?" Durga remained silent, her eyes ablaze. Mahisha took her silence as encouragement. "Hear of my greatness," he boasted. "I am King of Demons and feared by the gods. I hold control of the Three Worlds in my arms! You will never find anyone stronger than me anywhere!"

Durga kept silent. The buffalo demon considered that perhaps he would be more attractive to the goddess in a human form, and so he transformed himself. He bowed on one knee, like a suitor. "Your beauty, O Goddess, intoxicates me. Will you be my bride?" Durga, impatient with his babbling, became restless. Her weapons began to quiver, but Mahisha did not notice. "I will make you my royal queen and fulfill your heart's every desire. Together we will rule the universe!"

With a wry smile, Durga replied, "If you are so mighty, then show your strength to me. Fight me and win my hand in marriage."

When the buffalo demon heard this, he bellowed, "Do you not understand who I am? I am Mahisha, Lord of the Universe, who defeated Brahma, Vishnu, Shiva, and Indra in battle. You are but a mere woman. Don't provoke me or I will crush you like an insect."

"O foolish and vain asura," replied the goddess, "I am Durga, the invincible. I am the primordial foe of evil. I am the witness to all that is right and wrong. I protect the innocent and punish brutes like you. Prepare to die. No one can save you now!"

Durga then mounted her lion and advanced toward Mahisha and his army. The asuras hurled various weapons at her. She took a deep breath and exhaled—out of her breath emerged thousands of soldiers, who attacked the asura army. Her lion swatted the asuras aside like pebbles, killing thousands.

Mahisha seethed with fury. Since he was able to change shape, he first assumed the form of a lion and lunged at her, only to be thrown back by Durga's own lion. He then changed into an elephant and threw trees and boulders at her. Durga shot hundreds of arrows and shattered every object in mid-air. Her lion pounced on the elephant and gashed its forehead.

Finally, Mahisha assumed his true form, that of a giant buffalo, and charged at Durga, snorting and bellowing. A hurricane blew from his flared nostrils and swept away her army. He leaped into the air, ready to gore the goddess to death. But Durga was ready for him. She flung a noose around his neck. The more Mahisha struggled to free himself, the more the noose tightened. Durga jumped upon the buffalo and pinned him down. With her foot on his neck, she thrust her trident into his chest.

Mahisha attempted to abandon the buffalo body, issuing from its mouth with a sword, but he had only half emerged when the goddess, with a swift and terrific stroke, beheaded him. The evil Mahisha was no more.

The gods who witnessed this cataclysmic battle fell at Durga's feet. They prayed, "O Mighty Goddess, Upholder of Good, Destroyer of Evil, we humbly salute you! Mother of All, always be our protector and guide!"

Earth and heaven were peaceful once again. Goddess Durga laid down her weapons, assumed a serene form and said, "Go forth in peace, my children. You have my blessings, now and forevermore."

The lamplight flickers upon the pauranika's face, and a thought now flashes in her eyes. She recalls the debate between the boys and girls who came to visit this afternoon.

"So," she says, "it is all the gods together, as a unity, who give Durga her power. They could not defeat the Buffalo Demon without her, but would she have been able to defeat him without them? Remember, I said you might both be right, yes?" She could hear a few of the boys and girls restarting their debate.

"The Goddess Durga is created by the fire of righteousness, because justice and good always prevail. Even our small lives are a battle for this same victory, aren't they? Our best self over our brutish greed? Fighting against injustice whenever we come upon it?" She sees some heads nod in the moonlight. "Just as kings of old have counted on Goddess Durga for victory in war, so do we call on her in our difficult times."

Ganesha and the Mango

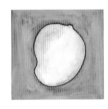

Lord Shiva and Goddess Parvati lived on Mount Kailasa with their two children, Ganesha and Kartikeya. Kartikeya was a strong and handsome boy, whereas Ganesha was pot-bellied, with short stubby legs, and sported an elephant's head. Both were brave, caring, and intelligent, and both loved their parents.

One day the mischievous sage Narada visited Mount Kailasa to pay his respects to Shiva and Parvati. After bowing to the divine couple, Narada presented them with a mango. He said, "Lord Shiva, this is a very special mango. It is sweeter than the nectar of the gods. Moreover, whoever eats it will become wise and learned."

Shiva thanked Narada for his gift and was about to cut the mango in half to give to his sons when Narada stopped him. "Stop, my Lord! Please do not cut the mango, as it would lose its powers. It is meant to be eaten by one person only."

Naturally, each brother wanted the mango for himself. They started to argue about who should be given it. Shiva and Parvati realized that the wily Narada wanted to test their sons and had set up this competition.

Parvati thought about it and came up with a solution. While the sage looked on, she said, "Whoever goes around the world three times and returns first will win the mango."

Kartikeya smiled. There was no way Ganesha could win this competition. Kartikeya's mount was a peacock while Ganesha's was a mouse. Furthermore, with an elephant's head, Ganesha could not dash about. Sure he would triumph, Kartikeya ran to his peacock without a word and started his flight around the world.

Ganesha knew well that he could not run faster than his brother, nor could his mouse match the speed of Kartikeya's peacock. As he wondered what to do, he had an idea. He hurried toward his parents.

Meanwhile, Kartikeya circled the world three times and returned, ready to claim the mango. Much to his amazement, however, he saw the mango in his brother Ganesha's hands. Bewildered, he turned to his mother. "How could Ganesha have completed the race first?"

It was the sage Narada who replied: "Ganesha claimed that his parents were his whole world. He asked Shiva and Parvati to stand together and circled them three times. Thus he won the mango."

Kartikeya looked long at his brother holding the mango. He knew that his brother had beaten him fairly. Kartikeya smiled, proud of his brother's wisdom. Ganesha smiled back and offered his brother the mango.

From late July to late August, from the Arabian Sea in the west to the Bay of Bengal in the east, many women in South India honor the Goddess Lakshmi in a celebration called Vara Lakshmi Vrata. Hindus revere Lakshmi, the Goddess of Prosperity, throughout India and all year round, but this is her special festival.

Lakshmi, the pauranika, was named after the goddess by her parents. Now, in preparation for the Vrata, she makes a mental list of all that she needs for the celebration. To make the traditional sweets, she'll purchase sugar, cashew nuts, raisins, and chickpea flour from the local vendors. For the family feast, the village farms will provide a bounty of coconuts, sugarcane, limes, bananas, eggplant, snake gourd, jackfruit, and more. She will make a variety of dishes as offerings to Goddess Lakshmi.

Today, a few days before the celebration, the storyteller will travel to the nearby city in order to purchase a new sari for herself and new clothes for all the women in her family. She expects her brother, Renga, who lives in the city, to arrive in a few hours to pick up her and her husband, Krishna. As usual, Krishna rose early, breakfasted, and left to work with the men in the fields. He will return when Lakshmi sends word of her brother's arrival.

Before she leaves to shop for the Vrata, it is Lakshmi's tradition, with her granddaughter Lalitha, to make butter from their buffalo milk and then to clarify the butter into ghee. Sweet as well as delicious, ghee is used for eating and medicine all across India. She will carry the ghee as a gift from her farm straight to her brother's wife, Girija. Churning butter by hand and making ghee are time-consuming, thinks Lakshmi, but so is everything worthwhile. By doing these tasks with Lalitha, she teaches her granddaughter some of the benefits of patience.

"Nannamma, Grandmother!" shouts Lalitha, bounding into the room. "Here I am!"

Lakshmi raises her eyebrows, pretending surprise. "There you are, young lady!" says Lakshmi. "You're here so early that we'll do the morning prayers together! And since we will be churning buttermilk in a short while, we will pray to Goddess Lakshmi, she who was born from churning the Ocean of Milk."

Lalitha scurries over to the *puja* (worship) altar. The cabinet's small bells tinkle as Lakshmi opens it. She then lights an oil lamp as her granddaughter collects a little fruit on the counter for an offering to the painting of the goddess.

"When we look upon Goddess Lakshmi," says Lakshmi, "we are showing bhakti, devotion. We are looking at God and thinking about God, thankful for the true wealth in our lives: our family, a good harvest, our health, and a peaceful life." Both put their palms together in front of their hearts and pray. In the picture, Lakshmi wears a rich, red, silk sari studded with every kind of jewel. Gold coins stream from one of her four hands, another makes a gesture of assurance, and the third and fourth each hold a lotus flower.

"She is the goddess of all kinds of prosperity, and that means she reminds us that there is both material and spiritual wealth," says the pauranika. "To me, the lotus she holds is perhaps the most beautiful of all flowers on earth because it rises toward the light from murky swamp water. No matter how messy our lives get, like the lotus we should lift our minds again and again toward the light of wisdom, toward God."

After a minute, Lalitha says, "You know what I like best about her, Grandmother? I like best that she rides a great white owl that flies through the dark and sees everything. I bet Lakshmi is never afraid of the dark!"

The storyteller laughs, wraps an arm around Lalitha, and pulls her closer. "Then I think that whenever you are afraid, you should think of the goddess and her owl." They leave the cabinet open until the oil lamp flickers out on its own.

Her granddaughter on her heels, Lakshmi walks over to the kitchen counter, which holds a stainless steel container full of buffalo milk fat. Every evening, Lakshmi mixes whatever milk their buffalo gave that they did not use that day with a spoonful of yoghurt to sour it, and lets it sit overnight to make more yoghurt. In the morning, she scrapes the milk fat off the new yoghurt and collects it. After several days, she has collected enough to churn into butter.

Lakshmi takes the milk fat and heads toward the churner sitting in a kitchen corner. The pauranika gives her granddaughter a spatula to scrape the fat into the churning pot. Its brown walls are so thick that the inside stays cool to the touch, even in summer. Lakshmi then takes a small rope with two wooden handles and wraps it round and round the spindle above the bowl, leaving two lengths to pull back and forth to make the paddle spin in the pot.

When her grandmother rises to stretch her legs, Lalitha sneaks in front of her and settles into a squat. "I'll churn first, Grandmother, if you begin the story!"

"No, I'll start the story first and you churn."

"Hey, that's what I said!"

"Really?" says the pauranika. Lalitha giggles.

"All right, then." Lalitha grabs a handle in each hand and pulls first one side and then the other. Still new to the task and a bit jerky, she eventually gets a feel for pulling steadily and smoothly. Like the gods in the story her grandmother will now tell, she will be at it a long, long time before she can collect the prize.

Churning the Ocean of Milk

 At the very center of the universe, in the very center of the Cosmic Ocean, the Ocean of Milk, a shining mountain peak called Mount Meru stretches in every direction for thousands and thousands of miles. Its blazing peak outshines even the sun. Boulders of gold, silver, and precious jewels clutter its slopes, and lower down, thick forests resound with the whole symphony of life—the most delightful songs of every kind of bird, as well as the roar and thunder of dreadful beasts of prey. Graced as it is by so much life—babbling brooks, flowers, magical herbs, and an infinite number of wishing trees—the gods naturally like to visit. However, no human being can ever approach it, even in thought.

Nowhere else in the universe does such an unstoppable fountain of life, vitality, and plenty exist. But what enticed the gods and demons to it most of all was that nothing on Mount Meru died or decayed. Neither the gods nor the demons had the power of eternal life, and they wanted it.

So an assembly of gods and demons gathered on a plateau of its slopes and conferred. The nectar of immortality had to be available somehow, by some means, and they wanted their fair share. After a time, Lord Vishnu suggested to Lord Brahma, "Let the gods and demons work together to churn the Ocean of Milk surrounding the mountain. It is exactly like a great churning bowl, and from this stirring, the hidden nectar of immortality will appear just like butter rises from buttermilk." Vishnu turned to face the assembled gods, saying, "Churn the ocean, O Gods and Demons, and you will be given the gift of immortality!"

Thus the gods and demons flew from the heights of Mt. Meru and made their way back to earth, to a great mountain called Mandara. This was to be their churning stick, extending as it did for thousands of leagues above the earth, and thousands of leagues below.

But first, they had to uproot the mountain. Using all their assorted powers, they pushed and yanked and shoved. Indra's thunderbolts, exploding at the same moment around the mountain's base only caused pitiful earthquakes. With all his might and breath, even Vayu, God of Wind, could not budge the mountain. By and by, the gods and the demons working together gave up, unable to detach Mt. Mandara from the earth. Despairing, they came to Lord Vishnu and Lord Brahma and petitioned them in earnest: "Lords, we don't want to ever die! Think of some way to pull up that mighty mountain for our welfare!"

Vishnu then instructed his mount, Garuda, the mighty eagle, to lift the mountain until it dislodged. The great Garuda grabbed the mountain with both his claws and pulled hard. When the mountain ripped from the earth with a roar, the gods and demons together brought the mountain to the shore of the Cosmic Ocean. But when they tried to place it in the ocean, the huge mountain, having no support, wobbled dangerously from side to side and began to sink. Seeing this, Vishnu acted immediately and took the form of a giant tortoise. Plunging deep into the ocean, he bore the mountain on his back to stabilize it.

The mountain was to be used as their massive churning stick and the thousand-hooded serpent, Sesha, as the churning cord. Sesha wrapped around the mountain and the demons grasped the serpent's head, the gods its tail. As the gods and demons pulled the snake back and forth, flowers and magical herbs from the mountain fell into the ocean. Mount Mandara whirled and twirled about so that even the largest trees spun off and fell from its slopes. As hundreds of thousands of trees rushed by each other into the ocean, a fire was born of their friction, and soon the mountain burst into a riot of flames and smoke.

The gods then complained to Brahma, "We are terribly tired now Lord, and all of us—gods and demons—have churned for a very long time yet we have no nectar of deathlessness in our hands."

Brahma turned to Vishnu and said, "Give them renewed strength, O Lord, as you are the last chance that they have."

Vishnu agreed, saying, "I give strength to all who help with this activity. Churn the Ocean of Milk all together. Spin Mt. Mandara round and round." Thus heartened again, the gods regained their strength and stirred the milk even more vigorously than before.

Initially through the renewed churning, great treasures arose from deep within the ocean. The first to rise to the surface was Kamadhenu, the sacred cow that grants all wishes. Appearing after that, lumbering but very dignified, was Indra's mount, the great white elephant Airavata. Then, swift as a thought, Ucchaisrava, a white horse, emerged out of the liquid and immediately leaped to its arc in the sky.

But next to emerge was Halahala, a deadly poison—the impurities in the ocean. It was so powerful that the devas and asuras began to choke on its toxic fumes. They quickly sought the help of Lord Shiva, God of Destruction, who drank the poison to protect the universe. Had not his partner, Parvati, grasped his neck to prevent the poison from entering his body, the whole universe would have been destroyed.

Then came the moon shedding its peaceful, milky light. And then, rising to the surface of the Cosmic Ocean of Milk, came the most important treasure of all, Maha Lakshmi, or Great Lakshmi. The gods and demons stopped their churning, dumbstruck. Dressed in white, she glowed, radiating holy light, while from her hands streamed torrents of every kind of wealth, too brilliant for any mortal to look upon. Goddess Lakshmi embodied the abundance of life, and her blessed presence was felt by one and all like rain on thirsty ground. Even the sun halted its chariot when she appeared until she took her place beside Lord Vishnu as his equal partner.

Nevertheless, intent upon winning the nectar of immortality for themselves, the gods and demons soon turned back to their work churning. At last emerged the Physician of the Gods, Dhanvantari, holding a single golden pot of the nectar.

When the demons saw this treasure they grabbed it and shouted, "It is ours, ours!" and began to line up to drink it. Immediately, Vishnu, all-knowing, saw that the demons' gain of immortality would prove catastrophic for the cosmos. Vishnu thus changed himself into a beautiful young maiden in order to bewitch the demons' minds with desire. So when the maiden, Mohini the Enchantress, smiled at the asuras and reached her fine hand out for the pot, they gave it to her gladly.

Meanwhile, the gods had also lined up to drink the nectar. The beguiling maiden, Mohini, turned around and gave them each a sip. By the time she was done with her task, not a drop of nectar remained in the pitcher for the demons. Mohini understood that the asuras would use it not for good into the world but only for their selfish aims. The maiden then took back her original, immense form as Lord Vishnu in order to ready for the battle she knew would be coming.

Knowing that they had been entirely cheated, the demons erupted in rage. In a flash, a great war between gods and demons began, the greatest ever fought. Iron darts, stone-pointed javelins, and other weapons flew through the air by the thousands. Those wounded by knives, spears, and maces fell to the ground. Demons' bodies, smeared with blood, lay in a crimson mountain. It was not clear who would win—the gods or the demons.

In the thick of the fight, Vishnu called forth his golden discus, Sudarsana, which subdues all asuras. Bright as the sun, it was unconquerable, terrifying, and glorious at once. It hurtled from the sky into Vishnu's hands, and he threw it toward the asuras with all his strength. It blazed through their ranks like doomsday, slaying them by the thousands. The remaining demons then scurried away deep into the earth, terrified as they were of Sudarsana.

So the gods won the battle—this time, at least. The gods put Mount Mandara back in its proper place on earth and traveled around the globe as water-bearing clouds, bringing life back to the bruised and scorched land. The gods won both immortality and the greatest treasure of all, Maha Lakshmi, the partner to Vishnu in sustaining all life. That life continues, that one season follows another, and that earth feeds us again and again is her miracle.

While the pauranika tells the story, the buttermilk in the churn forms a beautiful, golden mass. They both scrape it out and bring it into the kitchen, for now it must be clarified into the real reward, ghee. The stove is lit, the pot placed squarely on it, and after a few minutes, the butter boils and foams. As the story concludes, the foam subsides and forms a clear, golden liquid.

"Grandmother?" asks Lalitha. "Because your name is also Lakshmi, when you were a child, did you believe that you might be the goddess?"

Lakshmi laughs. "Perhaps I secretly hoped. And only for a very little while. When I was young, I was so excited for her festival day that I could barely sleep. I was very spoiled and very loved—a lot like you! I finally understood that my parents considered me their greatest wealth, and so they honored me with the goddess's name."

Nodding in understanding, Lalitha asks another question. "Grandmother? Does the Ocean of Milk have waves if the gods and demons don't churn it?"

"Oh, that is a fine question, Lalitha. You are seeing an important point in the story! The sages say that the Ocean of Milk is like our minds when we are very content and calm—like when we meditate. But when we want something too much, or wish something to be different than it is, that's the snake of desire demanding this or that, yanking us this way and that, churning the ocean into great and perilous waves."

"Like my cousin Rama, who took sweets without permission?"

"Exactly!" says Lakshmi with a smile. "Exactly. Desire causes us to do things we are not supposed to do."

Once the ghee has cooled and solidified, Lakshmi seals the containers. Lalitha jumps down from her chair and runs for the door, for she has heard the sound of a car.

As Lakshmi tidies up the kitchen, images of her mother, grandmother, and great-grandmother appear in her mind's eye. Of the many creation stories told across India, the churning of the Ocean of Milk is her favorite. It has been passed down by the pauranikas who came before her and is now written on her heart.

When her brother's beagle, Othello, races through the house with Lalitha in pursuit, Lakshmi playfully scolds the naughty dog. She can hear her brother Renga laughing, happy to be back in his ancestral village. It is time to go shopping for the Vrata, the festival celebrating Goddess Lakshmi.

The Well Digger

Once, a man in a small village set out to dig a well on his land. After selecting a suitable spot, he cheerfully set about his task. Although he toiled hard for hours, digging a hole deep as the height of his hut, he found not a trace of water. Tired and hot, he decided to relax for a while under the shade of a nearby tree.

As he was resting, a neighbor came along. "What have you been up to, my friend?" he asked.

"Digging a well," replied the man. "I have been digging since morning, but there is no sign of water."

"Oh! How I wish I had passed this way earlier," said the neighbor. "I would have told you exactly where to dig. Anyway, come with me. I know the perfect spot."

So saying, the neighbor led the man to a different place, assuring him that he would strike water in just a few hours.

The well digger cheerfully set about his task again. Hours later, after he had dug a hole twenty feet deep with no results, another neighbor came along.

"Digging a well, are you? What on Earth possessed you to dig here, of all places? Let me show you a better spot," said the helpful neighbor, and he got the man to follow him to a third place.

The neighbor pointed. "This is it! Dig here and you'll soon have water gushing out in torrents!" So the man began to dig a new hole. He dug, and dug, and dug, only stopping when night fell. This hole was over thirty feet deep, and still he saw not a drop of water.

Fed up, he muttered, "Thirty feet and the only water gushing out in torrents is my sweat! I am sick of digging!"

As he gathered his tools to go home, a friend came by and heard the whole story. "You can imagine my frustration," said the exhausted well-digger. "I have dug sixty feet altogether, in three different places!"

"Sixty feet!" his friend exclaimed. "If you had dug a sixty-foot hole in one place, surely you would have struck water by now!"

Despondent, the man made his way slowly home. "My friend is right," he muttered to himself. "I will stick to one spot tomorrow, no matter what anyone may say."

Krishna and the Serpent Kaliya

 Once, during an unfavorable world cycle, the asuras won a round of battles over the gods. As a result, injustice, terror, and disorder reigned on earth. The very processes by which life renews itself were under siege. Weak with poisons, drought, and fires, Aditi, Mother Earth, could bear it no longer. Her last chance, she knew, was to petition the Assembly of Gods for help.

To Brahma and the others she said, "My Lords! My lands are overrun with howling and shrieking demons. They swarm over all my beautiful works and set them afire! They fill my rivers with their poison so that even the seas now sicken. Forest by forest and hill by hill I am undone. Save me!"

To this plea Brahma responded, "O Celestials of the Assembly! We know that life is subject to ever-changing turns between good and evil. Let us proceed to the abode of Vishnu on behalf of Aditi, our Mother Earth."

Brahma then sank into a deep meditation, by which he communicated with Vishnu. "O Highest of All," thought Brahma, "take mercy on our Mother Earth! She begs your help. Earthborn demons are consuming her bounty! O Lord of the Universe, tell us what to do!"

In response, Vishnu plucked two hairs from his head, one light and one dark, and said, "These two hairs shall descend to earth as two avatars, human incarnations of divine beings. Additionally, all the gods and goddesses, each with their unique powers, must go down to earth and help. Only in this way will Mother Earth be rescued."

Out of these two hairs were born two brother-saviors. The fairer and older was named Balarama; the darker and younger, Krishna. They spent the happy years of their youth among the village cowherds. Playing in the woods and fields, they were able to hide from enemy demons.

The brothers did not reveal their divine nature, but Krishna, the younger, amazed those around him with his antics and feats. Wherever Krishna amused himself, even in the scorching heat of summer, the meadows would be as green as if it had just rained. He liked to dress up in shiny ornaments and tie his hair in a knot atop his head with a peacock feather stuck in it. Dancing and prancing through the forest, Krishna would look over his shoulder and see a line of creatures hopping and prancing right behind him.

Krishna was also known for his mischievousness. Once Balarama rushed home to tell their mother, Yashoda, that Krishna had put all manner of foul muck and mud in his mouth to eat. Worried and upset, Yashoda went to find him. Krishna claimed he'd done no such thing. "I have eaten no mud, Mother," he promised.

"Let me see for myself," she said, and opened his mouth wide.

What she saw struck her with wonder and awe: In Krishna's mouth she could see the earth and its creatures, the sky, the oceans, and the entire whirling universe, for Krishna was none other than Vishnu in the form of a toddler. "I must be dreaming!" she said aloud, and when Krishna hugged her, Yashoda's memory of the event vanished.

Krishna was so beloved that no one could stay angry with him for long. The village women complained to Yashoda that the boy had stolen their butter, but when they scolded him he simply giggled and ran away. "You should control that boy!" they said. Yashoda planned to punish him when he returned, yet when she saw his bright eyes and innocent face, her heart melted.

In order to see where help is most needed, superhuman avatars mostly stay disguised, appearing to be as caught up in the world as much as anybody else. Eventually, however, it becomes necessary to reveal their divine nature. So it was with Krishna one day a few years later, when he was forced to overcome the serpent king Kaliya, who had poisoned the waters of the great Yamuna River.

On a little expedition in the nearby hills, Krishna came upon a place in the river where the water boiled and writhed with flames. Trees overhanging the river were scorched and blackened from the fiery air. As Krishna looked, he saw a bird fall to its death just from passing through the fumes. All these signs showed Krishna that he had stumbled upon the notorious, multi-headed serpent king Kaliya. Because of this wicked snake, the whole Yamuna River, from Kaliya's den to the sea, was poisoned. Neither human nor animal could drink from it.

It is to vanquish evil that I was born, thought Krishna, and so I must go to war with this villainous snake! Without thinking further, the boy climbed the skeleton of a nearby tree and leapt into the water. Because he was an incarnation of Vishnu, Krishna's splash sounded a thunderous noise in the depths of the earth. Soon enough, Krishna's presence brought forth Kaliya, his eyes bulging red and wrathful, his hoods ballooning with fury, his fangs dripping with venom. Kaliya was instantly joined by hundreds of other serpent queens and warriors, one and all racing toward Krishna to bite him and wrap his limbs in their coils.

Alerted by the turmoil, a small crowd of cowherds gathered on the riverbank and watched in horror as their Krishna sank in the river unmoving and unconscious, weighted down and tangled in the snarl of a thousand snakes.

The cowherds ran back to the village for help. "Krishna, in a foolish fit of bravery, has jumped into the den of Kaliya. As we speak, the Serpent King devours him!"

Led by Balarama, Krishna's brother, the whole village ran to the river. When they arrived, Balarama found his brother lying limp on the bottom of the river. Women and children wept, for this was their beloved and fun-loving Krishna. "We cannot return to our homes without you!" they cried. "For what can the day mean to us, and what rest can the night bring without our beloved and beautiful boy?"

Then, knowing of Krishna's divine nature, Balarama fixed Krishna with the piercing eye of his inner vision and said, "Divine Lord, why do you surrender to human weakness? Have you forgotten your true nature? The universe is within your body, and within your body is the universe! Think of these villagers. You have pretended to be their babe and boy. Rise and show your infinite power!"

At these words, a smile worked its way across Krishna's lips, his eyes slowly opened, his limbs stirred, and his hands began to wrench the multitude of coils off his body. He burst forth from the tangle and trapped the Serpent King's head beneath his foot. And then Krishna did what he liked most to do—dance! Whenever he raised a foot in his jig, the serpent tried to wriggle free, but Krishna easily trod it down again with his other foot. At last, exhausted, Kaliya lay like a stick on the riverbed.

The smaller serpents gathered round their defeated king and said to Krishna, "O Ruler of the Universe, we recognize you! Please be merciful and spare the life of this our king!"

Kaliya roused himself enough to also beg forgiveness. "O Master of Gods! You have created me with strength and venom. I acted only according to my nature! If I had behaved in any other manner, I would have overturned the order of the universe and each creature's role. Have mercy on me! Spare my life and tell me what to do."

Said Krishna, "You must leave this river and forevermore make your home in the sea. My mount, the eagle Garuda, the arch-enemy of all serpents, will spare you and your kind in the sea if you do as I say." The Serpent King bowed at Krishna's feet, and he and his thousand serpent queens and warriors departed.

The waters of the Yamuna River soon ran pure, ending the thirst of all the creatures along its course. Very soon, the waters of Aditi, across all of Mother Earth, began to run clear and pure as she healed. Krishna, the boy hero, alert to the next challenge from the asuras, returned to his life of frolic among the cowherds, lavished with even more affection and praise by the villagers.

Because it is monsoon season, the children's spirits are as sodden as the ground. Puddles threaten to swallow any car braving the village dirt roads, and little traffic passes by these days. Everything drips on something or someone: the coconut groves on the buffalo, the mango leaves on the birds, the rows of tiles over the roof eaves on the people. The only creature enjoying the constant showers is the village elephant, tusks splotched with mud, now standing near the town's ancient banyan tree.

Thinking that a good story is the perfect remedy for soggy moods, the pauranika Lakshmi decides that she will gather the village children on her porch later this afternoon. Today being Sunday, a school holiday, the older children will want a tale to draw them in too. She has just such a story in mind, one about *maya*, the trick played upon us all our lives by the material world, the trick that each person must eventually see through to gain wisdom. Certainly, she muses, a story of maya will give those budding philosophers plenty to think about. The younger ones may not grasp it fully yet, but she is confident that a seed of understanding will be planted.

First, she needs to begin the day with prayers. She walks over to the shrine in the kitchen. The shrine cabinet is carved with holes that hold about a dozen small bells. Its door tinkles cheerfully. She always smiles at this gentle sound, waking people and gods from their night's slumber.

There are pictures and statues of several gods in the shrine, but today her prayers are to Vishnu. Since the story she will tell today features Lord Vishnu, Lakshmi recites several slokas in praise of him. Like all Hindus, the storyteller knows she can count on Vishnu's aid as long as she acts for the benefit of the entire world.

As she chants, she gazes at his image. He is a beautiful figure to behold: sky-blue, each arm holding an object to keep the natual order of the universe, the laws to which we are all subject, such as karma, the consequences of our actions. A shining disc of the universe circles one of his fingers, to be hurled at the enemies of good; another hand wields a golden mace to quash humanity's pride; a third hand bears a conch, the trumpet of sacred sound. The last hand cradles a many-petaled lotus flower. Because it blooms from the murky swamps, the large blossoms symbolize our potential for wisdom amidst our earthly conditions.

Finishing her prayers, Lakshmi steps outside into the courtyard, walks the short distance to her son's adjoining home, and asks her granddaughter Lalitha to invite the village children to hear a story on her porch that afternoon.

Some hours later, the pauranika has barely finished putting away the remains of lunch when two dozen youngsters make so much noise on her porch she cannot ignore them. When she steps out the door, the younger children flock like chicks around her feet. The older ones lean against the porch poles. As long as it doesn't rain too hard, everyone will stay dry.

The storyteller settles herself, closes her eyes, and chants a short hymn to Lord Ganesha. When she opens her eyes, she begins: "The Sage Narada, as you will remember, was a mythic wise man, a renowned teacher, a divine messenger, and also a notorious mischief-maker. Even so, the name Narada means one who imparts knowledge and wisdom to humankind."

Maya

 Narada was a great devotee of Lord Vishnu, and so he carried a *veena*, a stringed instrument, in his hand to continually sing Vishnu's praises.

One fine day, Sage Narada and Lord Vishnu took a long walk beside a river. By and by, Narada realized he had an important question to ask of the god. He stopped and turned to face Vishnu, who of course already knew the question to be asked as well as the answer. "O Lord," asked Narada, "what is maya?"

Lord Vishnu replied, "This question requires a rather complicated answer." He paused thoughtfully. "Before I explain, Narada, would you mind fetching me some water? The day is hot and my throat feels quite parched."

So Narada hastened to the riverbank with a bowl in hand. He was anxious to hear the Lord's answer. However, while kneeling on the riverbank to fill the vessel, he realized that he himself was quite thirsty. He put Vishnu's bowl aside, cupped his palms to collect the cool, fresh water, and drank his fill.

After Narada quenched his thirst, he looked up and saw a beautiful young maiden not far downstream, struggling to lift two large pots of water. Wanting to help, Narada rushed to her side and offered to carry the pots for her wherever she needed to go. Shyly, looking down, she nodded her agreement.

Narada filled the maiden's water pots, placed a small yoke over his shoulders, and heaved them up, careful not to spill. Following the girl, talking and joking with her, Narada forgot all about his heavy load—and all about Lord Vishnu, waiting at the river for him.

When they arrived at the maiden's village, her father, the headman, came out of his hut to greet Narada and thank him. But by that time, it was Narada who wanted very much to speak with the father. Smitten by the maiden's intelligence and beauty, Narada begged for her hand in marriage. The headman agreed on one condition: that she and Narada should live in the village, as she was his only daughter.

Narada and his new wife settled down by the banks of the river and built a house where they had many children. He became a wealthy farmer and even succeeded his father-in-law as the village headman. Loved by his wife, adored by his sons and daughters, respected by all the villagers, Narada led an idyllic life. When his children grew up and had children of their own, he found himself surrounded by dozens of grandchildren. Narada felt happy and secure. Nothing could go wrong.

Suddenly, above the village, clouds darker than a moonless night enveloped the sky, and for ten days thunder, lightning, and rain assaulted the huts and the fields. The river, swelling with the unrelenting rains and gaining speed, burst its banks and swept much of the village away. Narada's home dissolved like sand, and the floodwaters drowned everyone he loved and everything he possessed. He was only able to rescue himself at the last moment by climbing up a nearby tree.

It was then he finally remembered his god, Lord Vishnu. "Help me! Help me, Lord Vishnu! Please help me," he wailed.

Hearing Narada, Lord Vishnu immediately stretched out his hand and plucked him out of danger, away from the wild river. Narada, relieved and grateful, began to thank Lord Vishnu for saving his life. But Vishnu interrupted, saying, "But, Narada, I am still thirsty! You have been gone for over a half-hour. Where is my water?"

"A half-hour?" exclaimed Narada, weeping. "How is that possible? My dear wife and children, my home and all my possessions, my village—all the things I've loved over many years have just vanished! In the face of such disaster, how can you ask me for water?"

Vishnu looked at Narada with compassion. "Oh, Narada. You wanted to know what maya is? That was maya! Tell me, Narada, where did your family come from?"

Narada said nothing, and by and by Vishnu answered the question: "From me, Narada. Remember? Only one reality in the cosmos remains steady. Everything else is an illusion, maya, always in danger of slipping away. You, my greatest devotee, knew that, yet enchanted by life's pleasures, you forgot all about me, about God. You deluded yourself into believing that your material world was all that mattered. That, Narada, to be distracted for a lifetime from truth, that is maya."

Lakshmi pauses. Only a few water drops fall from the roof to the new-formed puddles below. She says, "Ah. The rain has ended as suddenly as it began!" And putting her finger to her lips, she tells the children, "Shhh. Listen."

Everyone is quiet for a few moments. "Like the rain," Lakshmi tells them, "everything in our day-to-day lives changes—sometimes in very big ways, sometimes in very little ones."

She takes the hand of her granddaughter Lalitha, who has managed to shimmy in beside her. In a soft voice, Lakshmi says to the group, "Who here has not been touched by this truth? Who has not lost something or someone precious? A grandfather? An uncle or aunt? A pet?" She knows their lives. News of hardship and illness is shared among neighbors, lightening their burdens. None of the children speak, but the moment feels comforting, like a soft blanket encompassing all of the villagers as one.

After a time, Lakshmi continues. "Vishnu reminds us to trust that a perfect, unchanging reality exists and that maya's display of form and color is merely a grand show. We lose ourselves and chase after this and that like a puppy after a ball." Heads nod. The storyteller laughs. "Sage Narada forgot this truth and lost himself in maya! So when you return home, please, each of you, stop by the temple and make a special offering to Lord Vishnu. Ask him to help you see through maya's flashy performance to the mystery behind it all, the Brahman that gives us life."

The skies are clear now, and the storyteller sends the boys and girls on their way. Children are all the sunshine I need, she thinks to herself.

God Is in Everything

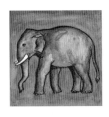 There once lived a *rishi*, a sage, so beloved he had dozens of followers. Wise and learned, the rishi taught his students the ancient truths, especially that God is everywhere—in each of us, in all creatures, in every thing that we see, hear, and touch. He enjoined his students to honor God day and night, for God is ever-present.

One day, some of the rishi's followers went into the nearby forest to collect firewood. As they went about their tasks, they suddenly heard a great snapping of branches and trees. Someone shouted, "Get out of the way! Run! A rogue elephant is charging through!"

All but one of the students took to their heels. That one, a young novice, stood his ground in a clearing and said to himself, "My teacher has taught me that God is in everything. I am God, and the elephant, too, is God. Therefore, we are one. I will have nothing to fear." Looking toward the commotion, he took a few deep breaths to calm himself and tried to appear welcoming.

A moment later, the elephant burst out of the tangle of jungle, spotted the boy, and headed straight toward him. The others, seeing his danger from their hiding places, yelled, "Clear the way! Clear the way, you fool! Clear the way!"

But the youth, caught up in his reverie, mused, "Should God be afraid of God? Why should God clear the way for God?" So he stood still, ignoring the shouts of the others to get out of the way.

Just as the elephant neared him, the boy bowed reverently before it. The elephant seized him with its trunk, picked him up, hurled him into the bushes, and continued on its way. The student was hurt and shocked, but eventually he recovered his senses enough to stand up and, with the help of the others, return to the rishi.

As the teacher bandaged the boy's wounds, out tumbled the account of his terrifying experience. Aggrieved, the boy said, "You told me that I was God!"

"Yes," answered the rishi, "and so you are."

"You also told me that all things are God."

"Yes," responded the teacher, "all things are indeed God."

"The elephant, then, was also God!" said the student, his voice rising in frustration.

"So it was," replied the rishi. "That elephant was God."

"Then why did it hurt me instead of bowing to me?" shouted the student.

The rishi paused in his work and, with a glint in his eye, looked at his young disciple. "My dear boy," he said, "while it is true that God was present in the elephant coming toward you, the God in all of your fellow students insisted that you should get to safety. Why didn't you pay attention to that voice of God?"

On Hinduism

The term *Hinduism* refers to a wide variety of native religious beliefs, customs, and literature that developed in India over thousands of years. The term was an attempt by foreign colonial powers to group these diverse practices together. Hindus prefer to call their religious systems *Sanathan Dharma*, which means "Eternal Truth" or "Eternal Path." With nearly a billion believers in India and around the world, Hinduism is the world's third largest religious tradition after Christianity and Islam.

Hindu myths and wisdom stories are told to help people engage with and understand life's intimate and ultimate questions, cope with its passages and challenges, live according to Hindu morals and precepts, and understand difficult philosophical ideas through art, ritual, song, dance, metaphor, and symbol.

Unlike many world religions, Hinduism has no spiritual founder (like Guru Nanak in Sikhism, the Prophet Muhammad in Islam, or the Buddha in Buddhism), no overarching religious authority (like the Pope in Catholicism), and no fixed set of beliefs or creeds (like the Nicean Creed in Christianity). Although Hindus still use many of the world's earliest and most beautiful religious texts, no single text is central to Hinduism in the way that the Bible, the Qur'an, and the Torah and Talmud are central to Christianity, Islam, and Judaism.

A belief common to all branches of Hinduism is that an all-pervading, all-sustaining reality known as Brahman underlies creation. Brahman is an eternal, imperishable reality that sustains all that was, is, and ever will be. According to Hindu scriptures, truth, awareness, and joy are fundamental qualities of Brahman.

The Hindu traditions are a way of life, with worship woven into the fabric of everyday activities. For instance, because Hindus regard all creation and all life as sacred, many are vegetarians. The prayer most often recited at a meal affirms that food is the energy of the Divine, being offered to grant us health and strength, wisdom and compassion.

Another belief common to all branches of Hinduism is that the cosmos and everything within it go through continuous cycles of birth, death, and rebirth. Hindus worship, pray, work, and seek wellbeing in this life and the next for themselves, their families, and their friends. Each person will experience the consequences of their actions. This principle of spiritual cause and effect is called *karma*. People's actions determine their karma; working hard, being compassionate, and doing one's duty generate good karma, meaning that the next life will be better than this one. Lazy, selfish, and wicked acts, however, produce bad karma and lead to poorer circumstances in the next life.

Hinduism is often described as a religion of thirty-three million gods. In some ways, it can be described as *polytheistic*, worshipping many gods. However, because all Hindus maintain the centrality of Brahman, the single underlying, Eternal Reality, Hinduism is sometimes considered *monotheistic*, worshipping only a single god. It can also be considered *henotheistic*, meaning that believers may focus their own worship on a particular god or gods, but they do not deny the existence of the others.

Hinduism does not attempt to achieve consensus or settle the question of who or what God is. Its goal is to give human beings the experience of God while acknowledging that each person's needs and approaches are different. Hindus are free to worship God in whatever way and form focuses their devotion and love. For instance, Hindus may choose to worship God as male (in such forms as Vishnu, Shiva, Rama, and Krishna), as female (in the forms of Devi, Durga, Shakti, and Kali for example), or as male and female together (as in the form of Ardhanareeswara, the union of Shiva and Parvati). They may envision God as a small child (Krishna), a man-monkey (Hanuman), an elephant-headed child (Ganesha), or a man-lion (Narasimha).

The many gods and goddesses are symbols of the one, absolute, all-pervading, imperishable, eternal reality, Brahman. Since Brahman is not easily grasped by the thinking mind, people ascribe specific qualities to gods and goddesses in order to venerate and worship them. For instance, Ganesha embodies the ability to overcome challenges; Shiva encourages worshippers to develop selflessness; the fierce goddesses Parvati and Durga embody courage; and Lakshmi symbolizes purity and abundance. Hindus see an *idol*—a statue or painting of a god—as a physical representation that helps them focus and pray. An idol is a visual metaphor of an invisible divine reality. It serves the same purpose to a devotee as a flag does to a soldier in the army, emphasizing spiritual attention and effort as a flag focuses a soldier's valor and patriotism.

Brahma, Vishnu, and Shiva are the *Trimurti*, or Trinity, the three highest manifestations of Brahman. Brahma is the creator of the universe, who labors alongside his partner Saraswati, the goddess of fine arts and learning, and rests from his work on a lotus that emerges from Vishnu's navel. Vishnu sustains the universe, promoting order and good by incarnating himself as an avatar, a divine teacher, to save humanity when it is in trouble. His partner is Lakshmi, Goddess of Prosperity and Good Fortune. Shiva, God of Destruction, dances the cosmic dance that ends each cycle of creation. His partner is Parvati, Goddess of Power and Courage.

Hindu gods and goddesses possess magical powers and have the ability to bless or curse humans and each other. All can take different shapes at will. They are often depicted with multiple heads and arms to symbolize their various qualities and powers and their ability to influence many things at once.

The universe of Hindu mythology comprises the Three Worlds. The first world or realm is populated by *devas*, benevolent divine beings, and is known as Deva Loka or heaven; the second, the earth inhabited by human beings, is known as Bhoo Loka; and the third world, Asura Loka, is a realm populated by the harmful *asuras*. Hindu myths are full of conflicts between devas and asuras, but just like human beings, asuras aren't always bad through and through, and devas aren't always perfect and good; some asuras pray and meditate and some devas are petty and foolish. Hindu mythology sees the universe as a battleground of good versus evil, and thus the balance between the Three Worlds is always shifting.

Story Notes and Sources

The Miracle of the Banyan Tree

This wisdom story is from the Upanishads, one of the earliest spiritual texts of Hinduism, containing many of its core philosophies. The word *upanishad* literally means "sitting down near," bringing to mind an earnest and curious disciple sitting at the feet of a teacher in an intimate session of spiritual instruction. The Upanishads include some of the most beloved stories from the vast literature of Hinduism's earlier Vedic traditions. On the surface, these stories describe the daily lives of people in ancient India, but at a deeper level, they shine a light on the spiritual experience of all peoples, Hindu and non-Hindu alike.

The Egg of the Universe

The first creation myth told by the pauranika, the discussion between Vishnu and Brahma, is from the Kurma Purana, one of the eighteen major *puranas* (epics) in Hinduism. Every major Hindu purana includes an account of how the universe was created. The second creation myth, involving an egg at the beginning of creation, is from the Chandogya Upanishad.

The Dhoti

This story is adapted from one of Ramakrishna's parables, titled "All for a Single Piece of Loin-Cloth." Ramakrishna was a nineteenth-century Hindu mystic and teacher. Born into a poor family of the Brahmin caste in rural Bengal, he was not very interested in formal education. He was, however, a gifted artist and singer and spent most of his time listening to spiritual discourses by visiting saints and holy men. At age six, he had a mystical experience while watching a flight of white cranes flying against a background of dark, rain-bearing clouds. His lifelong search to understand and experience God led him to study the sacred texts of Buddhism, Sikhism, Islam, and Christianity, and to see God in all beings. His message of religious harmony and universal love still attracts many followers.

Heaven and Hell

This folktale is similar to a Jewish story of long spoons. It is passed down orally from one generation to the next in India. Hindu folktales often communicate difficult life lessons by describing a sage or wise man making a moral point through a parable.

Yudhishthira's Wisdom

This story is taken from the Forest Section of the great Hindu epic, the Mahabharata. The Mahabharata is the story of a feud between the families of two princely cousins—the five Pandavas and the hundred Kauravas—to gain control over a large kingdom. Through deception and treachery, the Kauravas (led by Duryodhana, the eldest son) cheat the Pandavas (led by Yudhishthira) of their rightful share. When peaceful negotiations led by Krishna fail, the Pandavas are left with no other option but to declare war against their cousins. The culmination of the epic is the battle between the two families, which is described in the Bhagavad Gita ("The Celestial Song"). This text contains moral and ethical teachings to help a person lead a righteous life.

Lord Kamadeva, God of Love

This story is adapted from R. K. Narayan's *Gods, Demons, and Others*. The original story appears in the Shiva Purana, a religious text dedicated to Lord Shiva, the God of Destruction. The purana praises the glory and greatness of Shiva, describes the rituals and philosophies of his worship, and recounts his incarnations and exploits.

The Barking Dog

This story is adapted from Sophia Lyon Fahs's *From Long Ago and Many Lands*. It has both Hindu and Buddhist origins. In this version, Krishna, the eighth incarnation and avatar of Vishnu, comes disguised as a hunter to oppose injustice.

Shankara and the Outcaste

This story is based on the Maneesha Panchakam, a poetic dialogue written by the famous eighth-century philosopher Adi Shankara describing Shankara's encounter with Lord Shiva, who was disguised as an outcaste. Parts of the story are adapted from a traditional *Theyyam* performance in the southern Indian state of Kerala. Theyyam is a ritual form of worship that conveys moral lessons and social messages through music and dance; it is one of the oldest mystical art forms, dating back more than fifteen hundred years. The Theyyam performance used here was recorded by William Dalrymple in his book *Nine Lives: In Search of the Sacred in Modern India*.

The Birth of Ganesha

This story is adapted from an oral version that is told to children during Ganesh Chaturthi, a festival celebrating the birth of Lord Ganesha. Stories that are passed down orally from generation to generation tend to evolve and change. Variations of this one are found in the Ganesha Purana, the Shiva Purana, and the Mudgala Purana. Ganesha is one of the most popular gods of Hinduism, but the way he is depicted in Hindu art varies from region to region. In South India, where our pauranika lives, Ganesha has an elephant's head, a boy's body, four arms, and a potbelly. Always alongside him is his trusty companion, the mouse Mushika. As he is God of New Beginnings and Remover of Obstacles, Ganesha is worshiped at the beginning of any ritual or event. Endowed with a gentle and affectionate nature, he is also known as God of Wisdom, and he is the destroyer of vanity, selfishness, and pride.

The Wise Girl

This story is from the Chandogya Upanishad. In the Upanishads, we often come across *rishis*, sages who, in their search for truth, worship one god or another, but ultimately consider the object of their worship to be the Supreme Being, Brahman. Their mistake in not recognizing the divine in all things is usually brought to light by a god disguised in human form or by a child. This story is an abridged and adapted version of one in which a young boy teaches an important spiritual lesson to two rishis.

Chaitra and Maitra

This wisdom story is an expanded version of a *Theyyam* song recounted in William Dalrymple's *Nine Lives: In Search of the Sacred in Modern India*. This cautionary tale points out that we need to take care what we fill our minds with.

Indra and the Ants

This story is taken from the Brahma Vaivarta Purana and the Krishna Janma Kanda, adapted by Heinrich Zimmer in *Myths and Symbols in Indian Art and Civilization,* edited by Joseph Campbell. It gives a sense of the Hindu view of time. Hinduism holds that time is not linear; rather, it consists of cycles called *yugas*. The universe moves through a cycle of decay followed by pristine renewal. These cycles occur over vast swaths of time, like those conceptualized by physicists, cosmologists, and geologists.

The Wise Minister

This folktale is adapted from a collection of stories about Birbal, an advisor in the court of the Mughal emperor Akbar (1542–1605). The stories portray Birbal as witty and wise, using his intelligence to outwit his opponents, including the king. Stories involving a king and his sharp-witted minister are common in Indian folklore.

The Story of Goddess Durga

The Devi Bhagavata Purana is one of the most important texts of Shaktism, a branch of Hinduism that focuses on worshiping the feminine divine. The work describes Goddess Devi as Mother of the Universe and contains stories of her various incarnations, including the tale of Durga and her fight against the buffalo demon Mahisha. This tale provides the mythological backdrop for the annual festival of Durga Puja, celebrated in West Bengal and other parts of eastern India. This story is adapted from the Devi Bhagavata Purana and from *Hindu Myths: A Sourcebook Translated from the Sanskrit,* with an introduction and notes by Wendy Doniger.

Ganesha and the Mango

This story is a retelling of a popular South Indian tale that demonstrates Ganesha's wisdom and deep devotion to his parents, Shiva and Parvati. Legends and myths associated with Ganesha are recorded in the Ganesha and Mudgala Puranas, said to have been composed in the fourteenth century.

Churning the Ocean of Milk

This is an adaptation of one of the most popular stories in Hindu mythology. One of the highlights of the story is the rebirth of Sri Lakshmi, Goddess of Prosperity, one of Hinduism's most beloved goddesses. The story appears in the Vishnu Purana, the Bhagavata Purana, and the Mahabharata. There are a number of ways to interpret the spiritual aspects of the myth. It is sometimes used to teach meditation. In the version told here, the thousand-hooded serpent Sesha symbolizes desire. The human mind without desire is like a calm ocean, but the invasion of desire churns our thoughts and causes storms and waves.

The various objects and beings that emerge out of the ocean during the churning represent emotions and psychic and spiritual powers gained in progressing from one spiritual stage to another. These powers must be used to help others. The fact that poison also arises in the churning shows that we must work to integrate both positive and negative parts of ourselves in pursuing enlightenment. And the participation of both devas and asuras signifies the need to harmonize both these aspects of our personality through spiritual practice. Spiritual progress leads to spiritual health, enlightenment, and abundance, as symbolized by Lakshmi.

The Well Digger

This story, of unknown origin, is a cautionary tale told by parents to children. It shows why it is important to pick a path in life and follow it with discipline, consistency, and commitment.

Krishna and the Serpent Kaliya

The Bhagavata Purana, one of the most highly regarded Hindu sacred texts, tells the story of how Krishna, an avatar of Vishnu, purified the waters of the Yamuna River, which had been polluted by the snake Kaliya's poison. In this popular myth, the young Krishna, living an idyllic boyhood, remembers his dual nature (human and divine) at the last minute and defeats the mighty serpent, making the river available to the people and cows, who are both beloved to him.

Maya

The Bhagavata Purana contains many stories of the various avatars of Vishnu and focuses primarily on the life and exploits of his eighth incarnation, Krishna. The story as it appears here is adapted from the version made popular by the nineteenth-century mystic Ramakrishna and collected in *The Sayings of Sri Ramakrishna*.

God Is in Everything

This story is adapted from *The Parables of Sri Ramakrishna* and describes the danger of taking something literally instead of in spirit. The nineteenth-century mystic Ramakrishna was brilliant at conveying spiritual truths through parables and stories. Many of his parables were drawn from the day-to-day lives of people who lived around him.

Glossary

Agni. The Vedic God of Fire, who consumes the sacrificial offering and carries it to the gods.

amma. "Mother" in Tamil and Telugu, two of the languages spoken in southern India.

Ardhanareeswara. A composite of Shiva and Parvati, a figure who is both male and female to signify that masculine and feminine energies are inseparable. Ardhanareeswara also represents the ineffable and genderless nature of the Divine. In Hindu iconography, this deity is depicted as half-male and half-female, split down the middle.

ascetic. Someone who has renounced the material world in favor of spiritual pursuits.

asura. A power-seeking being that opposes and competes with the gods (*devas*). The word is often translated as "demon," but asuras are not always wicked.

Asura Loka. The world or home of the asuras.

atman. The innermost essence in every being which is divine; the essence of life, identical with Brahman.

avatar. A human incarnation of a divine being.

Balarama. The older brother of Krishna.

Bhagavad Gita. One of the best-known Hindu religious texts, preserved as the sixth book of the epic Mahabharata. Its title means "Divine Song," and it is a spiritual dialogue between Krishna, representing God, and Arjuna, representing the human soul.

bhakti. A worshipper's love of and devotion to a personal god, whether formless or in a form such as Shiva, Vishnu, or Devi.

Bhoo Loka. The world or home of humanity.

biryani. A dish of rice, spices, vegetables, and sometimes meat.

Brahma. God of Creation in the Hindu *Trimurti*, the trinity of manifestations of Brahman.

Brahman. The Supreme Self, Ultimate Reality, which is beyond all form and description; the Essence of Life; the Source of all Being and Knowing.

caste. One of the four traditional social classes of Hindu society. The *Brahmins* are the priestly class; the *Kshatriya* are the noble or warrior class; the *Vaisya* are the merchant class; and the *Shudra* are the worker class.

dal. Dried split beans or lentils, or a stew made from them.

dalit. A member of one of the groups traditionally excluded from the fourfold caste system, who were formerly called "untouchables" or "outcastes." The word *dalit* means "oppressed" or "broken," and is used to refer to people who were once known as "untouchables" or "outcastes," the fifth class in Hindu society. Today, dalits make up 16.2 percent of India's population and remain the most vulnerable, oppressed, and marginalized communities in the country.

deva. A divine or celestial being.

Deva Loka. The world or home of the devas.

Dhanvantari. The physician of the gods and the god of Ayurveda, a system of traditional Hindu medicine.

dharma. Right behavior, the observation of duty, truth, responsibility, law, and in recent times, religion.

dhoti. A traditional men's garment, consisting of a single rectangular piece of unstitched cloth that is wrapped around the waist, passed between the legs, and tucked in again at the waist.

dosa. A warm crepe made of rice and lentils.

Durga. A goddess sometimes called "The One Who Is Hard to Reach," who is an incarnation of Shakti.

gana. An attendant of Shiva.

Ganesha. The elephant-headed god, the son of Shiva and Parvati, Remover of Obstacles. Ganesha leads the ganas and is honored at the outset of any venture.

ghee. Clarified butter, made by simmering melted butter until the water evaporates and the solids caramelize. It is used in cooking, traditional medicine, and religious rituals.

halwa. A slightly gelatinous Indian sweet made with rice flour, sugar, and ghee.

Himavan. The king of the Himalaya mountains and the father of Parvati, the partner of Shiva.

idli. A steamed cake made of rice and lentils, a popular traditional breakfast dish in South India. It is typically served with coconut and cilantro chutney and *sambar,* a spicy lentil-vegetable stew.

Indra. The Vedic god of heaven, wielder of Vajra, the thunderbolt.

jalebi. A popular Indian sweet made of wheat flour batter that is deep-fried in pretzel shapes and soaked in sugar syrup.

Kailas. The mountain abode of Shiva and Parvati.

Kaliya. A poisonous snake living in the river Yamuna, defeated and banished by Krishna.

Kamadeva. God of Love and Desire and symbol of the creative impulse. He is shown as a handsome young man who shoots flower-arrows that induce love in their targets.

kamandalu. An oblong water pot, usually with a narrow spout and made of brass, wood, or dried pumpkin gourd. It is a symbol of asceticism in Hinduism.

Kamadhenu. A cow-goddess with the power to grant wishes, generally depicted as a white cow with a female head, breasts, and wings. All cows are venerated in Hinduism as embodiments of Kamadhenu.

karma. A person's actions, work, and behavior, and the physical, mental, and spiritual consequences of these.

Kartikeya. The younger son of Shiva and Parvati, Ganesha's younger brother. He commanded the gods who killed the demon Taraka.

Kashyapa. An ancient sage, one of the seven main sages in Hindu mythology. He is the son of Brahma and the father of Indra.

Kauravas. "Descendants of Kuru," a legendary king who is the ancestor of many of the characters in the Mahabharata. The hundred Kauravas brothers, led by Duryodhana, the eldest, lost a great battle against their cousins, the Pandavas.

Krishna. "The Dark One," the eighth incarnation of Vishnu but honored as supreme in his own right. He is a partly historical figure whose teachings are preserved in the Bhagavad Gita, and he appears as a hero and adviser in the Mahabharata.

laddoo. A ball-shaped sweet made of fried chick-pea flour, sugar, and ghee, often served at festivals and special occasions such as weddings.

Lakshmi. Goddess of Prosperity, Auspiciousness, Wealth, and Fortune; the partner of Vishnu; an incarnation of Shakti.

lassi. A sweet yoghurt drink.

Mahabharata. "The Great Bharata," one of the two great Hindu epics. It describes the war between the five Pandava brothers and their hundred cousins, the Kauravas.

mandap. An outdoor pavilion-like structure with pillars located in the Hindu temple complex.

masala dosa. A warm crepe made from rice and lentils, stuffed with potato and onion curry.

maya. Illusion, the mistaken perception of the material world as permanent.

Mushika. "Mouse," Ganesha's mount.

Namaste. A respectful greeting that means "I salute the Divine in you."

nannamma. "Father's mother," paternal grandmother.

Narada. A son of Brahma and ardent devotee of Vishnu, Narada is a Vedic sage who appears as a busybody in many Hindu stories to instigate the plot or drive the drama. He is depicted holding the *veena*, an ancient Indian stringed instrument.

Om. An ancient sacred syllable representing the breath of life, the sound of the universe; the holy word that represents Brahman.

Pandavas. "Sons of Pandu," the five brothers whose epic battle against their hundred cousins, the Kauravas, is recounted in the Mahabharata.

Parvati. An incarnation of Shakti; the partner of Shiva and mother of Ganesha and Kartikeya.

pauranika. One who is learned in the Hindu epics and puranas and gives discourses on them through music and dance. These events are usually held in the temple on special occasions, or in people's homes.

peeta. A short, rectangular wooden stool.

puja. A Hindu way of showing reverence to a god through prayers, chants, songs, and rituals. An important part of puja is making a spiritual connection with the divine through an image or icon believed to be filled with the deity's cosmic energy.

Prana. "Breath of Life," spirit, a name of Vayu, God of Wind.

Purana. A collection of ancient stories and parables that preserve traditions of cosmology, myth, legend, and ritual practice, and that teach spiritual, ethical, philosophical, and moral values.

Rama. The seventh incarnation of Vishnu, honored and worshipped in his own right. As a virtuous king, he is a symbol of righteousness and virtue and the and hero of the epic Ramayana.

Ramayana. "The Story of Rama," one of the two great Hindu epics. It tells the story of Rama, his wife Sita, and his victory over the demon Ravana.

Rati. The wife of Kamadeva, God of Love.

Rig Veda. "Hymns of Knowledge," the oldest and most important of all Hindu scriptures, containing 1,028 hymns to the gods of nature.

rishi. A sage who considers Brahman the ultimate object of their worship.

samsara. The cycle of birth, death, and rebirth.

Sanathan Dharma. Eternal Truth or Eternal Path, the name preferred by Hindus for their religious systems.

Saraswati. Goddess of Learning, Wisdom, and the Arts, the partner of Brahma.

Sesha. The serpent on which Vishnu rests. The word *sesha* means "remainder"; it is what remains after the universe is destroyed and out of which a new universe is created.

Shakti. Divine energy or power; a term applied to the Mother Goddess, either alone or as the female companion of one of the male deities.

Shanti. Perfect, transcendent peace.

Shankara. A name of Shiva; also the name of an eighth- or ninth-century philosopher who developed the philosophical system *Advaita*, which holds that God and humans are one, and who established monastic traditions that have since kept Hindu philosophy and mysticism alive.

Shiva. The God of Destruction in the Hindu Trimurti, the trinity of manifestations of Brahman.

sloka. A traditional Hindu verse or couplet consisting of two sixteen-syllable lines. It is the main verse form of many Hindu epics.

Sudarsana. The discus-like weapon with serrated edges used by Lord Vishnu. He is usually shown holding it in the right rear hand of his four hands.

tapasya. Deep meditation, a sustained effort to achieve self-realization, sometimes involving asceticism and solitude.

tilak. A small decorative mark on the forehead.

Ucchaisrava. a celestial white horse created during the churning of the Ocean of Milk.

uddharini. A long metal or wooden spoon used in Hindu rituals and ceremonies.

Upanishads. A collection of philosophical commentaries on the Vedas, parables, and wisdom stories. The word means "sit down near," referring to a student sitting by a teacher. There are about two hundred Upanishads, of which thirteen are the oldest and most important.

Vayu. The Vedic God of Wind and Air.

Vedas. Ancient Hindu scriptures containing chants, prayers, hymns, rites, and rituals. The word comes from *vid,* "to know." In addition to their spiritual value, the Vedas provide a unique insight into everyday life in ancient India.

Vishnu. God of Preservation in the Hindu Trimurti, the trinity of manifestations of Brahman. Vishnu is said to have incarnated ten times to vanquish evil and reestablish good. He is one of the most widely worshiped Hindu gods, especially in his major incarnations as Rama and Krishna.

Vishvakarman. The divine architect and carpenter of the gods, who built their cities and fashioned their weapons.

Vrata. A festival, religious vow, or act of devotion that may include fasting, praying, or pilgrimage in order to receive divine benefits.

yaksha. A powerful guardian spirit who protects a city, village, lake, or well.

Yashoda. Krishna's adoptive mother.

Yudhishthira. The eldest of the Pandavas, renowned for his commitment to truth and righteousness.

About the Authors

SARAH CONOVER's interests lie in building bridges of understanding between people of differing world cultures and wisdom traditions. She holds a BA in religious studies from the University of Colorado, an education degree from Gonzaga University, and an MFA in creative writing from Eastern Washington University. She has written six books on world wisdom traditions and the spiritual education of families, and published her poems and essays in a variety of literary magazines and anthologies. As a former high-school teacher she strived to bring multicultural perspectives to her students by collaborating with other educators worldwide. She was the recipient of two U.S. State Department grants that brought U.S. teachers to the Middle East to initiate classroom collaborations between students in the two regions. Before becoming a teacher, she was a senior television producer at Internews, an international NGO committed to fostering open media throughout the world. Sarah lives in Spokane, Washington, where she teaches creative writing and Buddhist meditation. This is her seventh book.

ABHI JANAMANCHI was born and raised in South India and moved to the United States in 1994. He is a third-generation member of the Brahmo Samaj, a liberal Hindu reform movement with ties to Unitarian Universalism. He has a BS in physics from Andhra University and an MDiv from Meadville Lombard Theological School. Growing up, Abhi heard many of these stories from his mother, his grandparents, and other adults around him, and they nurtured in him a lifelong love of Hindu stories and a passion for storytelling. He has been involved in international interfaith and multicultural work for over two decades. From 2006 to 2008, he served as president of the UK-based International Association for Religious Freedom (IARF) , the world's oldest interfaith organization. His Unitarian Universalist–Hindu faith, his Indian heritage, and his American citizenship inspire and guide him in this work. He and his son, Abhimanyu, are co-editors of *Falling into the Sky,* a volume in the *inSpirit* series from Skinner House Books. Abhi currently serves as senior minister of Cedar Lane Unitarian Universalist Church in Bethesda, MD.

About the Illustrator

SHANTHI CHANDRASEKAR is a Maryland artist who has been drawing and painting since early childhood. Her interest in understanding different media has led her to experiment with sculpture, photography, printmaking and papermaking. She has also been trained in the traditional art form of Tanjore-style painting. While many of her works are influenced by her Indian heritage, her true inspiration comes from the mystery and majesty of the world around her; her muse lives where the scientific overlaps with the spiritual.

Shanthi's works have been displayed in a variety of locations through the Washington D.C. area, and she has won numerous awards. She won the Maryland State Arts Council Individual Artist Award in both 2013 and 2016 for Works on Paper. She was awarded Individual Artist grants from the Arts and Humanities Council of Montgomery County, MD, in 2009, 2013, and 2016. She also won the Maryland Traditions Master Apprentice Award to teach Kolam drawing in 2010.